THE INFINITE REHEARSAL

By the same author

DA SILVA DA SILVA'S CULTIVATED WILDERNESS

THE EYE OF THE SCARECROW

PALACE OF THE PEACOCK

THE TREE OF THE SUN

THE GUYANA QUARTET

CARNIVAL

ff

THE INFINITE REHEARSAL

Wilson Harris

faber and faber
LONDON · BOSTON

First published in 1987 by
Faber and Faber Limited
3 Queen Square London WC1N 3AU

Photoset by Wilmaset Birkenhead Wirral
Printed in Great Britain by
Redwood Burn Ltd Trowbridge Wiltshire

British Library Cataloguing in Publication Data

Harris, Wilson
The infinite rehearsal.
I. Title
823'.914[F] PR6058.A692
ISBN 0-571-14885-9

FOR MARGARET,
HELEN AND CHRIS

NOTE

W. H. has stolen a march on me and put his name to my fictional autobiography. So be it. I do not intend to sue him for my drowned rights. Call it character licence on his part.

He and I are adversaries, as my book will show, but we share one thing in common, namely, an approach to the ruling concepts of civilization from the other side, from the ruled or apparently eclipsed side in humanity.

Not that my grandfather, my mother Alice, my aunt Miriam, or my close friends Peter and Emma saw themselves as ruled or afflicted subjects of an imperial establishment. And their voices, their plays, their dances and the theatre they created are immanent substance in this book. Yet my grandfather's *Faust* (which he wrote or brought to completion in the year I was born) possesses roots as much in the modern age as in the pre-Columbian workshop of the gods and therefore addresses a European myth from a multi-faceted and partly non-European standpoint.

All of which goes to show that my family were profoundly concerned with the original nature of value and spirit and for them there was no final performance to the 'play of humanity' or the 'play of divinity'.

Each apparent finality of performance was itself but a privileged rehearsal pointing to unsuspected facets and the re-emergence of forgotten perspectives in the cross-cultural and the universal imagination.

Robin Redbreast Glass

ONE

Let me begin this fictional autobiography with a confession. The values of a civilization – the hope for a universally just society, for the attainment of the mind and heart of love, the genius of care – are an impossible dream . . .

I repeat 'impossible dream', impossible quest for wholeness. In the same token, however, I *know* that those values are true and that the impossibility of their achievement nurses, prompts, gives reality to the creative imagination and instils one with profoundest paradox, with insight into the numinous character of all things, all features, all aspects of being.

Indeed I find it essential to trace the burden of value within apparitions that seem virtually irrelevant to moulds of prosperity, the apparition of the numinous scarecrow, the numinous victim, who (or is it which?) secretes himself, herself, itself in our dreams.

It is in the obvious partial being of the scarecrow – half-thing, half-person – dangling between daylight consciousness and the nightfall of civilizations that we sense a light (is it the light of remorse or of self-confession?) which may consume our biases and deposit fabric linking us to the extremities of humanity. For I know that the scum of the world cannot be divorced from myself or from my body in creation.

I know that in unravelling the illusory capture of creation I may still apprehend the obsessional ground of conquest, rehearse its proportions, excavate its consequences, within a play of shadow and light threaded into value; a play that is infinite rehearsal, a play that approaches again and again a sensation of ultimate meaning residing within a deposit of ghosts relating to the conquistadorial body – as well as the victimized body – of new worlds and old worlds, new forests and old forests, new stars and old constellations within the workshop of the gods.

Thus it was that I welcomed Ghost, conquistadorial and victimized Ghost (was (s)he male/female? I could not tell) when IT appeared on a beach in Old New Forest (a lofty beach hovering somewhere within south and central and northern Old New Forest) not far from where I earned a subsistence wage as a grave-digger in a library of dreams and a pork-knocker in the sacred wood. I decided to accept IT as male persona and trust that new fragile complications of divinity's blood would drive me to see the phenomenon I had encountered in the wholeness of a transformative light bearing upon all genders, all animates and inanimates, all masks and vessels in which a spark of ultimate self-recognition flashed . . . faded . . . flashed again.

Modern phenomenon or ancient magic? He (Ghost) wore a long, rich plait of hair on the back of his neck. It was covered with glittering salt from the sea and immaculate grime from a comet or from the stars. It was so long and marvellous it could have been the wonderful text of a woman's hair through which to read the mysterious birth of spirit.

(I need to be as accurate as I can in this fictional autobiography in order to balance uncertainties with a spectre of wholeness that has become the ironic substance of pure science in intercourse nevertheless with the impurities of wisdom and art.)

The graves I dug were libraries of myths of gold, silver, bone within a community of convertible soils and dreams that appeared in my Sleep, the living and the dead, texts of space travel, texts of sea travel, texts of the sacred wood, texts also of descent into the foetus, into the new-born and the unborn, descent into famine, texts that broke a uniform narrative domination by the conquistadores of history in inserting themselves into my book despite the apparent eclipse they endured, despite voicelessness or oblivion.

In regard to my status as a pork-knocker that is easily explained.

'Is there anybody there?' said the Traveller,
  Knocking on the moonlit door . . .

When I was short of food I tended to ascend oblivion's ladder as if it were a fat shoestring to the moon. I scrambled around for a morsel of pork hidden in a pale moon-barrel. I would *knock* the bottom of the upturned moon-barrel until a splinter of silver roast fell to my feet. In compensation for such largesse from the invisible host of the moon I dreamt of palatial halls and feasts of civilization, feast days, feast nights, of the sacred pork-knocker wood.

I was buried up to my lips in the bounty of hollow moon-roast (the fat shoestring dangling in my eyes) when Ghost appeared out of the sea. He clung to a moon-spade in the pit in which I lay, a sun-paddle as well on the brink of a setting wave, all this and more cemented into the ancient pen or quill of the sun with which I wrote.

Sleep was the terrain of blind/seeing comedy, the terrain of the moon and the setting wave and the sun.

In the wake of Ghost – as he scrambled ashore – lay a great, tall wreck of a ship battered and ribbed and gaping and glistening in the setting sun like a quicksilver goddess's hatpins in steep, elongated disarray.

Ghost had survived the assault of the sea in discarding his female hat and was emaciated and strange in a suit of gravity's anti-gravity string; and yet it was the life of the body that struck me (hollow yet inexhaustible body), the mesmeric quality of artery and vein on the moon, on the setting sun, on the black earth of Old New Forest sacred wood.

I was filled with the *naïveté* of intensest longing and love: was this an apparition of the resurrection of the body?

I saw the new moon like a curved fingernail in the late, afternoon Old New Forest sky. I stared at it with intensity. As if my hollow voyager lost and lost and found again and again had pared it from ancient Homer's webbed hand with immeasurable Joycean delicacy and drawn it on the sunset sky. Webbed Homeric hand. Impossible human bird. Impossible male, female animal. NIGHT WAS FALLING. My own fingernails were black with earthen light. I had been digging into a library of bone. Ghost approached me through my own pared extremities of Shadow and spoke in a foreign tongue (a mixture of vernaculars it seemed, bawdy verse and waste land poetry). I was baffled. Seeing my difficulty Ghost desisted and ceased to speak. Dumb Ghost. Illiterate Ghost. I was angry with him and with myself. I could not tell whether in playing dumb he wished to take on himself the constellation of a deprived humanity, deprived of dialogue with its innermost and fragile origins and with banished cultures of a half-sacred, half-profane truth. Was Ghost mocking himself or mocking me by taking upon himself the burden of an illiteracy of the imagination that plagued an age bordering Skull in the wake of lost quicksilver beauty and spiritual gold?

Perhaps his quicksilver genius verged upon values that were alien in spiritual substance to crass bounty, crass gold. And yet I *knew* him and he knew me through sober soil and self-confessing bone. Should I hand him over to the police or to the immigration officers (dressed as great sailors, great admirals) who patrolled this section of beach between the north and the south? Ghost read my thoughts and shook his head.

NIGHT WAS FALLING FAST and I led him up the quaking ground that shook with the impact of the sea into the house in the sacred wood where I lived. A lantern glowed there in the heart of starred bone, starred butterfly. We slept it seemed on the pillow of a wave. I dreamt with the dust of the ocean in my eyes of the coming of dawn. An immigration officer – Frog his name was – arrived at my door and knocked. Frog had the reputation of an inferior Don Juan Ulysses. He was accompanied by one of his painted mistresses, a black, white woman whose name was Calypso. (She belonged to the band of Tiresias Calypsonian Tigers whose fame had spread through many worlds.)

'Have you laid eyes on any fellow travellers around here, Glass?' Frog rasped. 'A blasted ship – pirates I bet from the moon – hit the reef here late afternoon. The reports on my deck or desk speak of one or two swimming ashore on a pin from God's hat that floated in a sea of hair.'

I shook my head in disbelief. Calypso was humming a famous bawdy ballad – STONE COLD DEAD IN THE MARKET. 'Don't play dumb, Glass. Yes or no?' Frog bellowed. Perhaps I should have said the same to Ghost! 'Don't play dumb, Ghost.' Or perhaps I should have offered him a drop of roast from the dream-barrel of the moon. A drop of roasted blood loosens a ghostly man's or a ghostly woman's tongue! A drop of blood truly reflected in the mirror of the self to nourish ancestral conscience may well have unravelled Ghost's speech when we met, and broken his silence, into words I could have read on the wall of the sunset sky. I had lost my head. I had not fed him. But surely the chance would come again. A chance to knock on the door of the moon again in search of every lost species in the oven of space. A chance to consume with Ghost a splinter of transubstantial creation in every chapel perilous of the heights and the depths . . .

Frog saw my distraction and faraway look. 'Say a pork-knocker yes or no,' he thundered like Admiral Ulysses Baboon. And then as if he too had lost his way and were distracted by untenanted worlds he whispered in my ear, 'Have you seen the axe fall upon the neck of the Old New Forest sun and moon economies? Has the industrial revolution of the sea given up its unemployed dead?'

I stepped back from him with loathing yet intimacy of scorched heart and mind. 'No,' I said at last, 'I have not seen any strangers or travellers around here.' I moved close to him again to reflect in the mirror of self the moth-eaten Skull tie he wore around his neck like an insect-spangled halter or noose.

As an inferior magistrate, as a piratical statesman, as an immigration great sailor or trickster officer, he could not help subsisting on a sea of griefs, on moth-eaten paradises. I understood (as I stared at Frog) another aspect of Ghost's dumb lips, Ghost's silence. For in mirroring Frog in myself it was as if the blood of the moon had turned to dead sea fruit on every political mouthpiece of my age.

Frog snapped at me now. He knocked on the door of my sea chest of books, and peered at the lantern-butterfly I carried within. He bared his teeth and his diamond-sharp eyes feasted on impossible glass in which he saw himself entangled in the multiple desires and waves of space and time.

'I hope for your own sake, Glass,' he cried at last, 'that you are telling the truth.' He turned away, mounted a parapet, and slid with Calypso into a battered ship of a car. As they drove away I tried to glance at myself as into the flesh of 'Glass'. One placated or withstood one's enemies or friends by reflecting their greed and offering it to them as the largesse of the moon. Much harder, of course, to reflect their virtues and astonish them as if manna were falling from heaven upon robin redbreast glass in the body of the mother of humanity.

Glass by name, yet lost golden species I was, lantern-butterfly or illuminated black pulse like a will-o'-the-wisp birthmark/ birdmark upon a page of the sacred wood.

Ghost was sitting on a bench when I returned to the book in which we slept. He arose and came close to me and his curious, wide-awake dreaming eyes appeared to comprehend the trials of inner and outer consumption of virtuous blood or greedy blood or dead sea fruit that had commenced. It was my trial as much as his. Should I continue to protect him, to shelter him?

WAS I STORING UP TROUBLE I COULD NOT FORESEE? Or would it lead to a revelation of the mystery of technologies of emotion in flesh-and-blood, complicated space virtues, complicated space greeds, threaded into human bias and the ascendancy of truth as sweetness or light yet bitterness or longing?

THE SEA BROKE IN MY TEETH. DROWNED TEETH. I DISLODGED A SPLINTER AND CLAMBERED UP THE STAIRWAY OF TIME INTO THE JAWS OF THE RESURRECTION. Ghost belonged. He may have appeared or risen in a sea-chanty book but he belonged to the oven of civilization: the burning sea; the oceanic fires; erosions and accretions. Belonged to the soil and the bone and the sea, to the butterfly page and to the lantern page, to the regime of the moth and to the derelictions of lust, to iridescent natures and to the gloom of planets with electric axes shining as if lit by primitive instinct.

The trial in which I was involved ran much deeper than simply concealing apparently illiterate Ghost from inferior Ulysses Don Juan Frog who patrolled the world in every national costume, east, west, north, south, Marxist, Capitalist.

NIGHT WAS FALLING FAST AS I TURNED A PAGE OF SLEEP AND WROTE: *Were the sailing men who circumnavigated the globe nothing but ancient chauffeurs, mechanics and technicians? Or were they so drunk with the spirit of value they had forgotten their motivation? Was God nothing but a giant chauffeur, a giant astronaut at the wheels of fire in space? Or did we need to read his ecstasy in the snake that takes wings and flies to heaven, the bird that takes scales and dives into the sea? Was the lamp by which the sun sailed nothing but a hollow fire? Or was it a light by which I dreamt my way backwards in time into the ancient workshop of the gods?*

In questioning those who sailed in drunken boats across the ocean to me, and to my savage antecedents long before I was born, I knew I questioned my deepest bottled instincts, deepest bottled intuitions, deepest bottled fears, deepest bottled hopes. I knew I questioned my savage antecedent of Old New Forest. Drunken Quetzalcoatl. Drunken wing. Drunken serpent. (I WAS ASHAMED I MUST CONFESS OF THE ECSTASY OF THE WING AND THE ECSTASY OF THE SNAKE, THE ECSTASY OF THE EGG FROM WHICH I HAD BEEN HATCHED. I WAS ASHAMED OF THE

POTION I HAD DRUNK IN SUBCONSCIOUS REALMS IN THE BOOK OF SLEEP FROM A SEED OF BLOOD IN THE YOLK OF SPACE.)

Drunken Quetzalcoatl was the source of all philosophy – the source of the hunt, the source of architecture – and in attuning his appetites to the mystery of the elements had coined the first vowel in evolution – curled egg-shaped snake coatl and curled egg-shaped bird quetzal – only to puncture or unravel the concept into a lightning shoestring potion, lightning artery, lightning vein, lightning intercourse between the rich and the poor, lightning mystery of deprivation as well as palatial conceits, lightning intercourse between himself and the woman of space, lightning mother of space from which he sprang into existence virtually without shelter, without food.

Had he forgotten the original spark, the original draught of ecstasy? Was this the source of his hunger, the source of his greed, the source of his guilt at divine incest? Or was it a measure of creative rehearsal, incompletion, half-spirit, half-flesh, elusive origins of unity, elusive origins of sex, elusive wholeness?

Ghost had nothing to say in reply to my questions except that I recalled when we had first met he had appeared to utter a curious bawdy confession that I had failed to understand. I had hoped he would tell me something however alarming, however incongruous, however chastening. But he had not. I had failed to comprehend. I had not fed him. Except with dead sea fruit that aped a spark of Homeric blood in the underworld of the twentieth century with its twittering shadows, its persecutions, its crucifixions. And I was left, therefore, to sense through his intricate gestures webbed with meaning – and the implicit masks he wore, the implicit disguises, deceptions – the immensity of bottled cargo he brought with him from every corner of the globe: not only bird-cargo, snake-cargo, but Christ-cargo, Socrates-cargo, male, female Tiresias cargo, ancient Egyptian, African cargo, modern, scientific European cargo . . . I was left to delve for the mystery of the resurrection from the bottled sea within myself, my intimate book. Bottled foetus in the body of the mother of humanity. Bottled seed in the black earth. Bottled page and bone upon which I wrote the music of the spheres.

The book of modern Europe possessed its roasted pigment in the adventures of Faust, Caliban and Magellan. It was a quantum book in which a particle of roast on the moon became a plunging horse saddled with all diasporas, all middle passages. Resurrection from a particle or a wave was a quantum saddle upon which a new physics rode into Bethlehem. I knew for in the country of Sleep I had seen a spade unlock a grain of sand into a towering beast of a wave upon which Ghost came with unwritten, written volumes for my library in the sacred wood.

I KNEW EVERYTHING. I KNEW NOTHING. I WAS THE SUBJECT OF AN INFINITE REHEARSAL OF A PLAY OF THE BIRTH OF HISTORY. Ghost slid from his towering wave of a horse in my library of dreams. He came to me with the head of Sir Walter Raleigh riding on his left hand. A giant El Doradonne brow upon which I read, 'History revises itself within the intervals of consciousness and unconsciousness that it takes for the economies of our age to fall again and again from the block and to touch the ground, consume a spark of dust, and rise into dream-orbit around the sun.'

I was dissatisfied with this. It was true. And yet it seemed too seductive, too charismatic. Ghost understood my dilemma and turned the brow of El Doradonne Economy around until it gleamed with the eyes of Prospero and I read in those pupils of brilliant dust:

'Revised spark. Revised histories of the world.' The brow darkened (NIGHT WAS FALLING) but cleared again into constellated peacock eyes and I read a ghostly script: '1832–3, emancipation of the slaves, the axe falls on plantation El Dorado. Landowners protest on behalf of the homeless, houseless slaves. Where will they go?'

THE BROW DARKENED. NIGHT WAS FALLING. BUT STILL I WAS ABLE TO DECIPHER A GHOSTLY FINGER OF INK. '1914–18. The axe falls on dynasties and privileges. Where will the unemployed go? *They march to the sound of a patriotic drum*. If you could see them as I do,

> My friend, you would not tell with such high zest
> To children ardent for some desperate glory,
> The old Lie: *Dulce et decorum est*
> *Pro patria mori*.

NIGHT FALLS BUT THE BROW FLICKERS AGAIN. '1939, the axe falls on Chamberlain's *peace in our time . . .*'

I could read no further but cried in desperation, 'WHY, WHY?' The brow relented and flashed a page in my book – 'Eat the Word of God in the twinkling of an eye when the axe falls and the Globe tumbles from the block to roll within the stars. Globe, yes, my El Doradonne globe in your heart, your privileged economy in my body which is susceptible to time's axe when systems are evil, the evil for which the innocent suffer. For the innocent (as well as the guilty) are you and me.

I was filled with rage. 'No,' I cried, pushing Ghost away, 'I shall hand you over to Frog. You are my conscience. I fear this quest for the nature and the meaning of value. Why must we axe evil and hurt ourselves? Evil is rich with prosperity and promise.' I stopped, filled with terror and shame. 'Don't pay any attention to me. I shall hide you, Ghost. I shall hide you in my Shadow. IN MY SHADOW. Where else?'

Ghost and I slept. Frog and Calypso appeared early on a page of shadow: page, yes, of the dripping sun that rains its ambivalent light upon the sacred wood. They kicked open my rusty book or gate and hammered upon the giant barrel I had built there to house a number of pork-knocker texts.

'Where are you hiding him, Glass?' Frog shouted. 'My information is that some God rode ashore here, near here, that the new moon darkened over the Middle Passage . . .'

'Christ!' I thought in some bewilderment.

'Don't look so damned outraged,' snapped Frog. 'I have my scouts. Some say they saw a man or a woman with a long plait of hair. Others say they saw a Beast or a Comet with a Snake around its neck.'

I could not help crying aloud in my sleep at Ghost's outrageous tricks and Frog's credulity. 'A snake around your throat is better than a moth-eaten cravat,' I said to Ghost.

'What's that, what's that?' cried Frog. 'If I catch Beast I shall interrogate him about the map of heaven. Do you hear me, Glass? It's my privilege. *I* interrogate strangers. I have built a traditional system and network. And another thing. I don't like you, Glass. You tangle me up in myself, in my own wildness, my own reflection *in you*. It's dangerous to see myself reflected in you, intimately black, intimately white. It's as if I have found the Beast of heavenly and hellish adventure in a subtle redbreast creature like you and do not know it. It's as if I'm in your dream. I may sentence you, I may judge you, but I'm an inferior at last. Poetic justice! You know me – you fleck of scum from the sea – much better, more deeply, irreverently, terrifyingly, than I ever knew *you*.'

I could not help shrinking a little at Frog's schizophrenic claws and diamond eyes that seemed to scuttle upon the mirror of a wave.

'I shall send you down, Robin Redbreast Glass, to the bottom of the sea. Do you hear me? I shall sentence you. I *have* sentenced you.'

'And I shall rise again,' I cried, 'into the map of heaven.'

I could have bitten Ghost's tongue in half. Had he spoken or had I? I had gone too far. Frog swung away and left me to ponder the sentence he had passed. The sea and the wood lightened into imminent Skull and Calypso began to hum 'Stone Cold Dead In The Market'. Then she stopped. Began afresh in a deep waving voice:

Belly to belly
Back to back
Ah don't give a damn
Ah done dead a'ready.

Don Juan Ulysses Frog was enlivened by the song. He returned to the gate to beat time with his fist on the pork-knocker barrel or drum. As he beat the sea responded and crashed into music. It was as if – despite everything – he had been transported to another world, a world unshackled from intrigue and treachery, the world of the map of heaven, the map of the Beast, the glorious Beast he wished to entrap from time immemorial. Indeed it was this steep longing – blunted, deformed – that had led him blindly into the uniform he wore as magistrate, admiral and immigration officer patrolling the beach of the sacred wood.

I had built the great drum or vessel of a barrel as a memorial to my grandfather who died in 1945 in the depths of Old New Forest sacred wood. I associated my grandfather with the early giant navigators who pork-knocked the high seas in search of the Beast of Paradise surviving somewhere, they dreamt, in the headwaters of time.

Sometimes becalmed in a wilderness of ocean reflecting a

jungle of stars and suns they prayed for miraculous beast-fish to nibble at their bait – a parcel of stellar beast-shrimp if nothing else – when provisions ran low and hunger stared them in the eyes in the Glass of the sea.

Belly to belly
Back to back
Ah don't give a damn
Ah done dead a'ready.

Calypso sang more deliberately – as if to supply longer intervals or spaces between lines than on the first occasion. This was astonishing as her song seemed to arise from the bowels of a slave ship becalmed a million light years from home.

Frog was suddenly discomfited. He ripped open the vessel or barrel in search of his Beast. He peered into the dark as into an organ of humanity. I walked over to him. My Shadow followed.

'The organ's a text,' I said, 'cinematic music, cinematic text. Calypso's lament with its implicit unshackled dead is as much about death as about self-abandonment, birth. It's a prelude to my grandfather's revised text of *Faust*. He read *Faust*, he loved Faust, and he re-wrote it in his own image. It was his last trip in the heartland. He was short of fresh fruit, greens, vegetables, and so on. Beriberi got him in the end. But as he starved by infinite degrees he tasted all the bitterness, all the sweetness, all the hope, all the despair in the world. And touched Faust the Beast. Faust the half-circus man, the half-mechanical soul. Faust of the womb and the grave. Faust the slave and Faust the self-mocking engineer of the gods . . .'

I was unable to finish. Frog was startled. His diamond eyes flashed with terrible jealousy and rage. All of a sudden he raised his mottled hand and before I could say Peter or Emma or Doctor Faustus or Beast or Angel he struck me a blow on the back of my neck. Poor Robin Redbreast, I thought instinctively, as blood flew through my Shadow and rested on Ghost's right hand. It was so sharp I felt the stillness of the blade pour and coil within me. My head toppled into the Globe. I saw the civilization of Skull and the Mountain of Folly that I needed to climb and transcend if I were to arise from the sea.

TWO

I was innocent. I was guilty. I was good. I was evil. I was solipsistic (autobiographical) character. I was polyphonic (fictional) author. Solipsistic (autoreflective) in seeking to mirror the frailest, deepest origins or unity of the self underpinning all creation. Polyphonic in reflecting alien voices, alien voices in familiar texts, internal/external counterpoint, deformities of spiritual gold and mystical silver, perversities of epic, blind rendezvous with Ghost, diverse masquerades, self-revelations, self-deceptions . . .

The many conflicting versions of the coming and the arousal of Ghost, the leaden-tongued yet silver-tongued expressions of Ulysses Frog (epic lover yet doomed, jealous scavenger of humanity), the dumb lips of Ghost, the lament of Calypso's unshackled dead, the country of Sleep that I inhabited as if I lay on a pillow of the ocean yet walked upon waves of land, the breaches of convention, the overturning of expectation, *were all the substance of chaos edged by* redemptive passion, redemptive hope, in the body of the resurrection that I reflected in myself as the price of an infinite rehearsal of value and spirit.

The sentence of chaos had been inflicted on all species the year I was born, 1945, the year the Bomb fell and history changed, revised itself backwards, never to be the same again.

FROG'S MOTTLED HAND HAD FALLEN LIKE AN AXE IN MY SLEEP. Fallen on many a reflected economy in Mirror and Shadow of Flesh-and-Blood in the flight of the crane or the swallow or the dove from north to south. Shadow-crane, shadow-dove, shadow-fish, with broken neck floating high on a wave or high on the land. I, Robin Redbreast Glass, flew headless then spun with a feather and a scale into the turning Globe, the turning wave, the turning hills, the turning valleys. Put my head and my hat on again and bowed in my Sleep to Prosperity's block and Necessity's block.

Capital block prosperity? I asked Ghost who flew in the shadow of a wave and a hill but his lips were sealed though a strange cry trembled in the recesses of coming Skull but remained short of utterance.

Marxist block necessity then? I asked Ghost: 'Tell me, Ghost – how deceptive, how real, are Necessity and Prosperity? Are they disguised ballrooms and cells of evil in which the heads of the unemployed roll? Are they in essence the polarizations of a Faustian morality that we need to untangle until the Beast smiles and points to heaven rather than to hell?'

I raised my hat to Faust as the flock of my terrors skimmed a wave and settled on the ground and in the belly of the sacred wood.

'We are reborn with the fish and the bird, Ghost. We are reborn through the sword that severs the umbilical cord and flashes in the light of the sun and the moon with sudden estrangement from a body of darkness, foetal terror revised, foetal hope revised, revisionary edges of subsistence upon light and darkness, subsistence upon the brute world, subsistence upon the bland world.'

The wood was in a state of alarm. And indeed I sensed a change in the disposition of the tenant in my Shadow. Ghost was alarmed and uneasy at the intrusion of brute climates, brute absolutes, in the communication of ideas under the sea and over the sea that Faust had converted into a machine, fish of steel, fish of lead, fish of iron, birds of steel, birds of lead, birds of iron.

The mechanics of the circus of power on sea and on land made Ghost tremble on his flying trapeze in the belly of the sacred wood, the mechanics of domination in the name of Brute Prosperity or in the name of Brute Necessity.

Was this opposition between Brute and Brute a prelude to an era of temptation in which one Brute devised ruses of tenderness and humour to tempt the Other? 'Bow down to me, dear fellow Brute, and the kingdoms of earth are yours. Save in the degree that I keep my options open to save the world and to bring you to heel.'

Faust – both Goethe's and Marlowe's – had been a priceless possession in my grandfather's stock of books. He was still mentally athletic and young when he died aged fifty-five in the heartland of the sacred wood. He had pored over Goethe and Marlowe nights under an uncertain fuel lamp after labouring days in the creeks of the rainforests that ran through his barred consciousness. Ran like a woman's fluid constellation born of the reflected moon and the reflected sun. Golden offspring born of the inimitable self-penetration of the reflected moon and the reflected sun. Such was the Glass in which he dipped his pen to write his own version of the Beast of immortality, the Beast of the circus and of the machine. I was there in that new version, the Glass child in the golden woman my mother. I was born (may I say it again) in 1945, the year my grandfather died. It was the year of the Bomb, the year of Nagasaki and Hiroshima. 'We are born with the dead, with the fish and the bird.'

I was the foetus revised, the unborn grandson revised, entangled in the waters of mirrored death revised in the unconscious fluid of my coming birth. There was a turbulence in that revised fluid and I *knew* what my mother knew. I shared with her – in a kind of void yet potent revisionary abstraction – her concerns, her anxieties, the postman's knock bringing letters from my grandfather in the distant heartland.

I knew he thought of us – and had heard of me – from the letters Aunt Miriam wrote to him and received from him, the letters my mother Alice wrote to him and received from him. I could not be sure in those turbulences when the dream of diamonds and gold gave way to me, to Glass, and he saw me like a fluttering redbreast bringing its hat (or was it its head?) to Faust and skimming the creek in which he dug for spiritual wealth as well as crass bounty. (Years later when I read his book I saw he had dedicated it to me, his unborn grandson Robin Glass.)

At first he would have given his soul, he would have bartered my head, Robin's head, for offspring of crass gold, for the diamonds in the eyes of Ulysses Frog that sometimes clouded mine as I slept. ('Frog's eyes,' my mother once said when we peered into the mirror together, 'are your eyes, Robin. No wonder you invent such terrible guardians of the beach.') He would have bartered his soul for crass gold, he would have bartered Ulysses' head in my self-loathing, self-reflecting Frog's mirror of the injustice of epic plunder, epic statecraft but was stopped. Something happened. He wrote to Alice and Miriam to say he heard voices singing 'Stone Cold Dead In The Market' and within those voices a whisper that may have been the faint voice of Robin Redbreast foetus revised in the book of humanity, the book of the Beast of heaven and hell, far up in layer upon layer of sleeping trees. It was the whisper of ironic singing temptation offering him elusive orchid-kingdoms worth a million, elusive toucan-kingdoms worth a million, elusive parrot-kingdoms worth a million in the zoos of the east and the west.

Elusive head of time as well. It was then he began to prize me, prize the ironies of strangest hidden conscience everywhere, the Glass of multi-reflecting telegraph of soul. I *knew* when he died because my mother knew. I tasted a melon or an orange on her lips. It tasted sweet. Whereas on his it had become a dry shell, the shadow of Skull, in the beriberi zoo that claimed his life. A strange animal he seemed to me at the end as I dipped within my mother's body into the script, the illuminated script, of her dreams. I saw him roaming the palaces of the peacock-orchid and the unicorn-amaryllis in search of his limbs as they crumbled into the fire and Shadow of Glass, my Shadow. I was a shadowy revised foetus and I gathered those limbs together into a giant dream, giant reconstitution and moved paradoxically upon a fragile arch. I was a shadowy Robin Redbreast revised Glass drifting by uncertain degrees towards a twin desolation or waste land through which to plumb the rebirth of my age.

That desolation, that dismemberment, was bland economic malaise indistinguishable from bland twin prosperity or from bland twin necessity.

It was a blandness I sometimes reflected when the Brutes hid their faces in my Glass. It was the blandness of a spiritual malaise, economic malaise . . . As though the mirror atrophied into a paradise without fruit . . . Was Faust in league with the bland, with the Brutes?

Before I could put the question to Mother or to Aunt Miriam or to Ghost a turbulence within the years since 1945 washed over me, over Glass, over Robin Redbreast, and I saw an incongruous feast of numbers, a new mathematics of the hollow soul. Bountiful numbers in a starving bland universe through which I flew with headless cranes and headless doves in my Sleep before settling again once more into the belly of the waving wood.

When did it first dawn on me in scanning the new *Faust* by my giant parent that he (my grandfather) was a mathematician as well as a poet of the magical dead? Take the following equation. *Giant* equals *pygmy* in the incestuous bomb of the divine. He had become a distant, unreachable giant when my biological father vanished and diminished in my consciousness into a pygmy. Distant giant yet close at hand in the turbulences I knew within my mother's flesh. I mixed them up (giant with pygmy) since I had seen neither; *that mixture was at the heart of all the fiction I was to write*; my pygmy vanished the night I was conceived, my giant died the day I was born but grew large as God nevertheless.

He was the God of the heartland who had sent pots of gold to us. He was an alchemist whose pay dirt was gold or the diamond eyes of Frog of whom I was to dream (Frog, the inferior shadow of the giant, Frog, the Don Juan trickster pygmy who resembled my vanished father) over the years of childhood, adolescence and maturity when I reconnoitred the beach of Old New Forest and waited for Ghost to arise from the sea.

It was God who inspired me not to be entrapped in a trauma of losses (or in the bounty of ill-gotten gains) but to build through Sleep the resources for a complex autobiographical fiction reflecting both execution and rebirth, holy/unholy parentage and the resurrection of the body built into inimitable being, inimitable species and masquerades of creation . . . I shall write of my mother later and the crucial part she played . . . indeed never ceased to play. How else could I have known the quantum womb, the quantum turbulences, through which Ghost came out of the grave of the sea?

That year, when my mother was great with child, my grandfather sent her the manuscript of *Faust* to read and to type. Then came the telegram. It was the end. *I knew.*

The staccato rhythm of the typewriter punctuated my sleep like muffled gunfire. Her heartbeat quickened as she read and typed. Commotion piled itself into commotion. The giant slipped from the mask of the Faustian poet into the mathematicians' code of nuclear rape. Did I dream it then or was it years later? Was it a recurring nightmare? I asked Ghost: how was I involved though still in my mother's body in a dream of pure poetry, pure mathematics, yet nuclear rape? Was I an internalized cipher in the corruption of 'pure' mathematics, 'pure' inner space God? Or an internalized gene in the corruption of the 'pure' humanities, 'pure' humanities God? Bland mathematics. Bland humanities.

Soulless machine. I asked Ghost. From faraway in the heartland, poetry and mathematics extended their fist to prod my mother in her ribs. Her contractions began. *The Bomb fell upon Hiroshima and Nagasaki*. She was rushed to hospital. I was born within the instant hour – or flash of eternity – the Bomb fell. I *knew* an anguish I could scarcely fathom. I attribute it now – that anguish – within the Glass of time and the Blast that happened to an effulgence of birth threaded into death, a white blistering fist or axe of light coming so close it was as if pure poetry and pure mathematics died in the instant I was born.

I bowed to my mother's ghostly legs as I emerged through them into the blinding light, the blinding axe, as they (poetry's glass legs, mathematics' glass legs) seemed to break and fold under her yet in other women's bodies reflecting my mother's, *through* other women's bodies reflecting my mother's. They gave birth to me even as she did.

A poem's glass legs, mathematics' glass legs, reflect the terror and the ecstasy of the new-born. New-born hubris in mirroring birth-in-death, death-in-birth?

'Not absolute hubris,' I said to Ghost. 'Surely not! Profoundest desire to unravel hubris I would say in a quest for original value, original spirit, in a dangerous world.'

THREE

Let me now confess to the gravity of finding myself face to face with questions I hoped to duck but which have been the substance of recurring dreams throughout my life and from the day I was born.

Old questions yet new.

Who am I? What is fragile humanity? What is poetry? What is science? Can they save creation in complex and ceaseless rehearsal of the birth of spirit? What is the value of survival – is it arbitrary chance or partisan mould – or does it open doors into innermost, self-reflecting and reflective being? Have I been asking these questions all along in this fictional autobiography? If so I need to return to them again and again, to sense new emphases, new edges, new extremities, new proportions.

Take the question of survival. Does survival imply an inner mirroring capacity in league with the magical dead who move in one's blood, the magical unborn who move through one's blood, magical yet tainted antecedents, magical giants, magical pygmies?

THE BOMB HAD FALLEN. Its consequences were with us into eternity. Nothing would ever be the same again. An awesome dream.

Where lie the roots of such hubristic knowledge in an infant such as I – infant mankind in infant womankind? Where lie the seeds of such peculiar transparency – the one in the other – such peculiar transparency enfolding all creatures? I find myself positing quantum legs, quantum glass in the building blocks of the universe.

Such astonishing and daring fragility that is susceptible to an inimitable self-reflection of all faltering achievement and power may still give us an edge or a particle or a grain of ascendancy over chaos and bring us abreast of the subtle race, the subtle shadow, the subtle and complex majesty of the genius of paradoxical spirit.

I BEGAN TO CLIMB THE MIRROR OF SLEEP THE MORNING I WAS BORN.

It is a source of incredible wonder – that borders on cruelty all the same (the cruelty of the innocent new-born in the guilty new-dead) to be possessed by a recurring dream of *accusation* through childhood into maturity, accusation that apparently starts from the day one is born, the *silent* accusation of the species.

BORN DEAF – the dream declares. THE BOMB IS FALLING. No music anywhere. The harps of the angels are numb or dead. But one climbs each silent string. Ghost was as silent as the glass robins hopping in my room, silent robins, amongst whom I stood. Silent unicorns. Silent seals. Silent blackbirds. Silent larks.

They had flown or run or swum on a wave into the room on the blast of the wind and the wood and the sea from pole to pole.

Glass Red Riding Hood lambs and wolves from the building blocks of the universe were loping into the room, transparent but scorched, across the windowsill. A glass unicorn in a building block within the staggered tenses of time, present and past. The unicorn is. The unicorn was. Not a bay. Not a sound. Not a horn. An eerie deafness, eerie silence, eerie destitution of music. THE BOMB FALLS.

Glass toucans perched on my cradle and pecked at my eyes and ears in the building blocks of the universe. Yet not a tap, not a hammer, not a nail, could break the silence in the Looking Glass space I had become. I was all reflected creatures flying on glass wings, swimming with glass wings, walking upon feet of glass in the building blocks of the universe.

I saw the dove's addiction to propaganda and to war enlarged into immutable plague, immutable silent discord, deaf mute of silence. I saw the tiger's susceptibility to false knowledge enlarged into immutable flame, silent discord, deaf mute of the sun. I could not hear or fathom its roar, its blaze. I turned to Ghost across the years and understood at last the cautions that had been threaded into his enigmatic and muffled tongue. He had been telling me of the silence and the deafness that would encompass my age if I failed to sound the origins of spirit. AND THEN WHEN ALL SEEMED LOST – WHEN I HAD SURRENDERED MYSELF TO TOTAL SILENCE – I REMEMBERED THE REVISIONARY *FAUST* THAT MY GRANDFATHER HAD WRITTEN AND THAT I HAD SCANNED WITH REDBREAST EYE AS MY MOTHER TYPED. I had been possessed of an eye, it seemed, that shone in her breasts, an ear that flowered in the tunnel of her body. I had swum within turbulences and reflected oceans of space. Not oceans now but bombed woods in this recurring dream with its whisper of temptation aloft in the trees at the heart of a chorus singing 'Stone Cold Dead In The Market'. Singing 'seize the species, seize the kingdoms of the earth, grab, plunder, possess.' It was then – as if there had been a clap of thunder in the grave – that my deafness vanished and I *heard* the bustle, the movement, the traffic of the kingdoms of the earth. *All mine, mine to seize.* I had been tempted by a whisper in the trees in my mother's body to 'seize the species, seize the kingdoms of the earth' and had responded instantaneously. Those kingdoms took the form in my dream of quantum, psychical glass, psyche's glass tigers, psyche's glass seals, psyche's glass unicorn (and all the other creatures that had loped or swum into my room) in the building blocks of the universe. I reached out to seize them and I *heard* the bustle, the movement, the traffic of time, as they slipped from my grasp.

I felt a complex guilt, a complex shame. And yet I was grateful, grateful to someone or something (whoever, whatever, had tempted me). I was glad that I had responded, that I had succumbed, that I had attempted to seize the kingdoms of earth and space. Yes, I had succumbed to the temptation but had also seen through the veil of the moment into the roots of life with which I moved with all creatures that one seeks to seize, the roots of strangest whispering transparency that is the seed of the listening heart in every self-confessional fabric of the birth of truth, the birth of creative conscience.

Was I glad, was I sorry, that the kingdoms of space had slipped from my grasp? I was glad. I was sorry. And within the nexus of such ambivalence almost forgot the whispering Shadow of temptation to which I had succumbed until I stepped with Faust into it, into that now bristling, telephonic Shadow. A telephone was ringing in my mother's heart or ear into which the creatures of glass had swum or run before they vanished into a whisper of music. I heard it distinctly whereas before I had heard nothing. I heard the clamour of church bells in the sacred wood. I heard them so mysteriously, so potently, it was as if a flock of mighty bell birds flew from down under and encircled the globe. It was so insistent, so wonderful, that I was seduced *by another curious and strange bell at the end of a long fishing rod which Faust held over my grandfather's creek in the sacred wood.*

'Faust,' my grandfather had written (I scanned the page with an eye in my mother's breasts), 'is the comedian of the kingdom bell. The fisherman-bell is the kingdom bell. The fisherman-king is the comedian of the machine. Pay attention please.' THE TEXT CONTINUED: Robin Redbreast's revised foetus, glass bird, flew in his mother's cinematic body and alighted on Faust's fisherman-rod. It (the cinematic foetus, tiny bird) settled on the rod, sidled along it with numb claws until it gained a foothold, a claw-hold, on Faust's kingdom bell. It fluttered its numb feathers and danced on the bell like kingdom come. The fisherman-rod swayed as it danced. The line descending from the rod dipped sharply in the water as if it had been bitten by a fish. The swaying and the motion were enough to awaken a multiple ripple on Robin's mother's belly. But the kingdom bell on the fisherman-rod did not make a sound. 'It's not ringing,' Robin protested, 'it should have rung to say that the fish in the water is biting . . .'

'You mean,' said Faust wryly, 'that you, glass Robin Redbreast bird, are dancing on my kingdom bell.' He stared into Robin's eyes.

Robin felt numb. It was as if his claws were seized by violent cramp even as they danced. They danced on the bell but felt nothing. Why did they feel nothing? Why had he not known the instant he *touched* the bell that it was devoid of a clapper and a tongue, that it was a *simulated* bell not a real bell? Why had he said 'a fish in the water is biting' when he knew (or should have known) the commotion came from his active perch or dance?

The answer lay in the riddle of *touch*, the riddle of the *dance*. It lay in the riddle of Faust's implicit dialogue between creatures, between hypothetical fish and numb foetus in the body of humanity.

'Note,' said Faust to Robin, 'in giving you claws, foetal claws, like a bird's, or a crab's, I enhance the ironies of the circus and the machine, I am true to fashion, true to obsessional creed and animal destiny in a harshly competitive age . . .'

'And what about spiritual destiny?' asked Robin. He felt heavy all of a sudden. 'Do we not lame or cripple animal destiny in equating it with human and competitive slaughter?'

'Tut, tut,' said Faust. 'Toot, toot, heigh-ho nonny and all that! So much for spiritual destiny.' But his eyes were glued to Robin's, fiendishly glued, spectacularly glued, and yet there was a crinkle of humour, even pitiful/pitiless understanding, at the edge of his lips.

Robin wanted to protest but he was mesmerized by Faust's extraordinary sophistication, irreverence and candour.

It was as if the cinematic atmosphere they shared crept into his blood and endorsed his lameness of mind and spirit even as he danced. Faust called the bell at the end of his rod his kingdom or dancing bell because without making a sound it spoke of a labyrinth of patent or invented process – patented flesh, patented bone – between hypothetical creature and cinematic humanity dancing in ballrooms of heaven rounded like great, clapper bells, dancing in space, in tune with the fabric or womb of mother earth but insensible to deprivation.

Faust was the master of new-born ironies and abortive spirit. His kingdom bell spoke of simulated dialogue between hypothetical God and hypothetical Man. It spoke of the bleak conversion (bleak exploitation) of deprivation into puppetries unconscious of hollow being.

Robin sought to protest again. 'There is life and death, death and life, and somewhere in that ambivalent mixture lies the spark of innermost recall of the value of spirit . . .' But Faust brushed him aside: 'Quite understandably,' he said, 'you assumed that when the line shook under my kingdom bell that it was life biting, that life had taken the bait or the hook. Hypothetical life Robin! Remember that.'

'I was wrong,' Robin acknowledged.

'Hypothetical life,' Faust repeated. 'Such is the measure of progress. We advance through spheres of deprivation by which we gain tools – have you forgotten the bristling noise of the telephone when you were able to hear?'

'I remember the secret music,' Robin was able to say though his tongue ached like Ghost's.

'We advance through spheres of deprivation through which we simulate the life of species. Take it a step further, Robin. Put your faith in material progress. Accept me as some kind of prodigious immortal. And then I will make you into my immortal prodigy, my born/unborn prodigy in the bottled but cinematic sphere of a woman's body. Your mother's body! Invent the mother. Invent the child. Let me touch you and begin the process.'

'No!' said Robin. He felt uncertain, bewildered, even vaguely outraged. He took refuge in attack – 'Let ME touch you.' He was uncertain of the distinction between touching Faust himself and being touched by Faust himself . . . MY GRANDFATHER'S BOOK FADED INTO THE REALITY OF IMMORTAL DREAM. I WAS DREAMING. *Immortal dream? Had I succumbed to Faust's temptation*? Could I touch him without being subject to his influence, his charisma? Had I involuntarily accepted the temptation he posed to sustain his immortality and to become immortal dream writer myself? What are the origins of dreams? Are dreams the relic of temptation surviving in the psyche to assume immortality? If so the burden and the ecstasy of dreams had to be revised, ravelled, unravelled, penetrated, probed, rehearsed into infinity in order to make a profound distinction between a true resurrection (*a true resurrection*) and the strings of prodigious dogma in populations. They resembled one another, they ran in parallel with one another (material prodigy resembled the body of the soul even as cinematic foetus resembled the innermost recall of the conception of life) *but they were not the same.* LIKE YET UNLIKE FORCES.

I reached out and touched Faust and felt suddenly *caught* in the nexus of like yet unlike forces, caught and bedevilled by an age that gestated at the edge of a chasm, the chasm of marvels, the chasm of insensible creed in the circus of the machine.

I felt devoid of sensation as I touched him. He felt warm at first, warm as the drug of material progress, but I knew he was bitterly cold, bitterly calculating, stuffed to the eyeballs with terrifying comedy. *All of a sudden I screamed.* It was wholly spontaneous but nothing could have been more calculated to take him by surprise. I should have been laughing my immortal head off at his immortal joke – he seemed to imply – *not* screaming . . . He had failed somewhere in the demonology of the circus to 'grab me' as I hopped on his kingdom bell and I knew in my heart of hearts the resurrectionary or revolutionary body was subtly alive however apparently eclipsed within the glamour and the sophistications of the comedian of the machine.

Whereas before I had been delivered from deafness by a clap of thunder in the cradle or the grave – when I sought to seize the psychical glass animals of space that were manifestations of the immanence of God's kingdoms – *now* in the circus of the machine, on the circus of the kingdom bell, I was delivered from numbness of spirit, and from seizure by Faust, with a cry I gave from the heart, a cry so poignant, so real, it drew me into the web, into the flesh, the imperilled substance, of all ecstatic and sorrowing creatures. Was this the origin of mental pain woven into the very substance and moment of rich rejoicing? Caught yet instinctively liberated feature. Caught yet spiritually liberated song.

I HAD BEEN CAUGHT YET IMPLICITLY LIBERATED FROM CINEMATIC CHARISMA, CINEMATIC ECLIPSE OF INNERMOST SELF-REFLECTION.

'The *mystery* of deprivation!' said Faust at last. As if with a gesture he sought to enlighten me, to prove he was on my side after all. On the side of liberation.

'I am on your side once you *read* me properly. With a literate imagination Robin!' He was laughing. I could not be sure. Was he laughing or was he mocking a world that was singularly ill-equipped to read its spheres of deprivation or its proclivity to temptation?

'To enter my Kingdom Bell is to see from the other side of thunder the earlier temptation to which you succumbed. I say 'earlier' but does one know what comes first, what is early, what is late? Does one *hear* before one *cries*? Is it a simultaneous arousal within veil after veil of rehearsed temptation, rehearsed sensation, secreted in memory?

'You succumbed to temptation and reached out to seize the glass unicorn, the glass tigers, etc. They vanished but you came alive then to the reflected thunder of all things, to the noises of space and time. At last you could hear, make distinctions, dwell in your mother's voice and her laughter. Now you yourself have been caught by me yet implicitly liberated in giving voice to a spirit through and beyond yourself . . . At last you *know* that you cry, that tears are as true as song. Have I not helped you in the very moment that I threatened your soul? For remember within true voice and true hearing lies an arch of simulated being upon which we build our architectures and institutions. There in due course you will come upon Skull and the bridge to Skull.

'At the heart of the void of the machine lies a revolutionary spirit that exposes one's zest for life within the fruits of temptation. That revolutionary spirit exalts us, yet chastens us, makes us see our deprivations (whether deafness or numbness or whatever) through a mysterious glass or composite of opposites reflecting seizure and liberation, invention and creation, the animate and the inanimate, the living and the dead, the mortal and the immortal.

'I am the comedian of the void in the machine . . . the void in you. I am the script within the machine.'

'And my voice?' I asked rudely, 'is that in your script?'

It was a taunting question to put to a human machine or to a person embodying immortal dynamo replete with implacable marvel and terrible skill, terrible dialectic, but Faust to my astonishment replied, 'Your voice is revolutionary spirit, Robin. I am glad of this, believe me! I too can rejoice.' Was he mourning with me or laughing at me or had he been moved in spite of himself by considerations of the *mystery* of deprivation and its bearing on caught yet liberated senses of the imagination, the mystery of deprivation through which we unlock multi-faceted thresholds, landscapes, doors into being?

FOUR

Some Reflections in 1985 on the Great Strike of the Animal Bands in the Magic Wood in the Year 1948. Ghost is at my Elbow as I Write in the Chapel Perilous of the Sea. He is the Spectre or Character of Time Unravelling Centuries and Decades.

THE MYSTERY OF DEPRIVATION. A key phrase in this fictional autobiography of (or is it by?) a drowned man. W. H. insists mystery is a divine comedy with an edge or positive direction to the movement of consciousness above the authorial fury of conflicting powers and the chaos of the world. Mystery is a stairway that takes me up yet back four decades in the comedy of time to the year 1948. I was three years old then. It was the year of the great strike in the sacred or magic wood. Memory's building blocks under the sea (or upon a wave of land) are composed of reversible glass senses reflecting patterns of intimate sensation – no, *patterns of temptation* – to which one succumbs. I would never have acquired a literate ear, or literate responses to distinctive voices and sounds – literate self-criticism as well about my deficiencies of understanding in every nexus of intricate being – if I had not been tempted by a stroke of light to seize the kingdoms of space that sped before me in inmost animal and spiritual particles and waves of sound. I would never have given voice to creation if I had not been tempted by the comedian of the machine to become an immortal dream-body upon frontiers of simulated blood and real blood.

I laugh at myself now in 1985 in the light of the composite fruit of temptation that stains the mirror of my lips. Glass kisses glass at the bottom of the sea where fish roam in one's hair like beautiful birds. My mother kissed me on the bed of the sea in the chapel perilous and said to a friend, 'Miriam and I thought Robin was deaf, you know, but suddenly he reached out and held my breasts, he heard my voice, the noises in the street, everything, the telephone ringing in the room. It was funny. He began to speak as if he were conversing with someone at the other end of the line. A prodigy! He cried . . .'

She was right. I screamed and woke. After that speech came naturally. It was born out of an extremity, yes, extremity, Robin's extremity, Redbreast Democratic Glass and multi-reflecting organ of the deprived senses. Yes, speech is born of extremity. It runs close to despair, demagoguery and authoritarian command, all functions of deprivation: deprivation or deprivations Aunt Miriam tended to call *illiteracies of the heart and mind.* I have never forgotten the phrase she used. It laps around me in the rain, in the water, in streams where one misreads time's face.

Aunt Miriam was right in that we soon forget how strange and mysterious are our capacities, hearing extremity, listening extremity, speaking extremity, touching extremity, seeing extremity, knowing extremity; and that those capacities or extremities may never have come into being except through a dream-life that is steeped in temptations – pre-natal temptations as well as child-temptations – sexual temptations as well as lust-for-power temptations – to which we succumbed. Succumbed yes to the vitality of sensation but recoiled in converting the shadow of temptation into a source of original, self-confessing being in creation.

I remember the terror of the animal bands when they faced the repetitive fall of the Bomb in the shape of perverse manna and Skull-bread. They erupted in the magic wood in 1948. First came the band of the Tiresias Tigers. They were followed by other bands that included the Unicorns and the Horses of the Sea. It was a strike of international significance. It invoked a bullish mood (whatever that meant) in that sugar cane shares rocketed and fell, rocketed again with stone cold dead in the market. Rice shares became animalcule balloons and bullets. Oil shares battled coal. Diamond and gold investments laced the bullet's horns. That a Tiger could stand on a platform (or a tall sheep or Red Riding Hood or Sister George the Bald Horse) toss a drum or a claw to the winds, and thereby cause millions of ammunition and dollars to roll up the creek, or roll down the creek, was a measure of economic illiteracy and of the deprivations of simulated cities of Skull.

'BOOM, BOOM, BOOM, DOOM, DOOM, DOOM, all the time,' my mother said. 'Enough to drive you mad!'

Aunt Miriam – despite her misgivings, her sense of spiritual malaise – was more generous. 'It's all in a good cause,' she said.

And pondered the uncertainty of good causes. 'Bang, Drum, Strike, to keep the evil spirits at bay.'

'What evil spirits?'

'Shame on you, Alice. You should know. The legacies of war. The legacies of fear and corruption. Malnutrition. It's a strike to win grain.'

My mother looked dubious, even doleful. 'Corruption,' she said. 'Grain,' she said. 'Vile bodies.'

Aunt Miriam was nonplussed. She could not tell whether Alice was saying 'corruption is vile' or 'grain is vile' or 'the strike of the animal bands is vile'.

'I tell you, Miriam,' Alice continued, 'it's the terror of the void. That's the twentieth century.'

'You mean the terror of angry and confused spirit,' Aunt Miriam said and tried to look absurdly reasonable though she was scared. 'The animal bands are dancing like nemesis below in the street. What a sea of faces. I hate crowds.'

A change had occurred in the element of Sleep. The privileged and fashionable strikers and bangers, privileged bands and dancers who preyed upon – or were able to exploit – the illiteracy of the economic imagination and move grain around the globe to starving peoples were dissatisfied with themselves and their entanglement in systems they both supported (profited from) and loathed (or bled in the name of the good cause). They swung around in the book of Sleep into rebellious subversives inciting masses. I sailed upon a tide of popular art, street animal dancers, street animal rebels, street animal poems of protest. Their simulation of an industrial and cultural strike seemed suddenly real. The comedian of the circus who pulled the strings and profited from each calculation of unrest had misjudged the chaos in the magic wood. Time's countenance darkened into a mirror of involuntary feud on the stairway backwards and upwards, forwards and downwards, upon which I dreamt I climbed.

'What is spirit when it broods upon chaos, Alice? Ask the politicians, the ageing politicians of the world, who are henpecked in the sacred wood. I ask *you*, Alice. I ask you to come on stage on the crest of a wave – the name I have given our little theatre.' (Aunt Miriam ran a school of drama (called The Crest of the Wave) in her home beside the sounding sea. It was but half a mile or so away from Alice's house in which many rehearsals were conducted.)

'Let's begin. Let's rehearse, Alice.' She stopped again as if she were intent on dramatizing the part she wished Alice to play. 'I ask again – what is spirit when it broods upon chaos? Don't reply straightaway. Shrug your shoulders and point to the Sphinx. Then say – let me see – something like this: "when angry spirit becomes an incestuous block or riddle the food in our very mouths is susceptible to plague".'

'I have no intention of saying anything of the sort,' said Alice. But this was her cue nevertheless in my sea of Sleep on the crest of a wave. She moved across the chapel perilous to the window on the waving street beneath our house. 'I say the terror of the void,' she cried in the heart of my dream. Her glass lips touched mine as fish flew through our hair like beautiful birds. 'I say the terror of the void. The terror . . .' and then she saw the spiritual (or the vile) dancer Tiger staring up at her from the street and listening intently. Her voice fell . . . 'of the void.'

Spiritual (or was it vile?) Tiger had heard every word. He leapt on the stage with his drum of thunder and his guitar. He leapt over the fence, raced to the front door and was inside in a flash. *And then I knew.* He had been manipulated by Faust, Faust's machines, Faust's technologies, to bang away at the terror of the void. My mother had pricked his animal spirit on the raw.

'What a paradox,' said Miriam. Her lips moved in the play that she and Alice had half-made-up, half-borrowed from my grandfather's *Faust* in the last days of his beriberi wilderness.

'What a paradox,' said Alice. 'This is the age of the masses, the age of the best-seller, the age of the popular arts, the popular bands, and yet it is the age of the death wish, the age of drugs.' Alice was nodding as if they murmured the lines together.

'The torment of spirit. The death wish of an age. True spirit never wars with true spirit but since nature and the values of nature are inextricably woven into every populace – and populace is vulgar spirit – every illness of mind and of spirit becomes the substance of bodily, addictive passion, bodily, addictive fury, ear-splitting, addictive BOOM, BOOM, DOOM, DOOM wrestling with itself for a violent/non-violent habitation.'

Then Tiger spoke the lines my grandfather wrote for him. Lines written in his last days in the Bush of the magic wood. My grandfather consumed the shell of a Skull-orange. It tasted so wonderfully sweet that he knew he had been deceived and that

Death, the Tempter, stood beside him with the lotus flower in his hand. No ordinary lotus flower. Not the luxuriousness and the inactivity of the grave. No, something much more insidious. Deprivation. The drug of deprivation that looks like the seed of black (or white) purity, the black (or white) seed of God, when the drummer of the senses protests in a fever against the ills of the world that are as much in him as in those he assaults. The lotus flower of addictive bias that hardens into terror! My grandfather chewed it, tasted it, knew its wonderful relish, then spat it forth into Tiger's speech.

'If I bang Ghost,' Tiger said, 'in a dead poet's – a dead magician's – shadow in the sacred wood I may grasp, may I not, the hidden malaise (and hidden revolutionary capacity) in the popular arts? I shall try to bang Ghost and make him talk to you, Robin. Make him unravel the masquerade of Death as the Tempter, the bringer of the lotus flower. It's a narrow pass, very narrow indeed, that I must take, I the dancer, the rebel.

'*You* dead poet, dead magician, dead Quetzalcoatl, dead priests and scientists of ancient time, understand – surely you do – the predicament of the popular yet doomed player, popular yet doomed rebel, in an illiterate world. You swing in a sea or a cradle where I blow my deadly trumpet that is wreathed still, I confess, in unawakened powers, unawakened sensibilities, and in the mystery of deprivations through which I must pass. *I confess to a reluctance to pass.* Such self-righteous deprivation, such pride, seduces me, fastens upon me, as if it were the seed of purity, the seed of God.'

Tiger had succumbed to the Tempter, to the lure and fallacy of black (or white) purity, and as a consequence the confused and confusing diet of the world, half-vile, half-spiritual, rushed into his Shadow and mine even in the last moments of his life, the ticking voice of the suddenly energized clock, ticking invisibly/soundlessly within the roar of passing time.

Tiger was dying though he had not yet realized it. He was dying within my grandfather's shadow on the page of a book in which history revised itself, the deprivations of Democracy and popular art revised themselves into cautionary ink, the dangers of fascist order, fascist purity, fascist white, fascist black. He knocked on the door of the page to elicit further lines from the dead magician's hand. My grandfather may have heard. His dead hand, the hand of the magical dead, responded. It wrote some lines that it recalled from its youth before I was born. It could not write its own lines at that moment so it leant on the riddle of the Traveller from another time. As much as to say 'you may knock Tiger and even though I hear I must be silent in order to stress that there are no easy answers to the predicament of a dying age within its most obvious, most telling biases and assumptions.'

'Is there anybody there?' said the Traveller,
  Knocking on the moonlit door;
And his horse in the silence champed the grasses
  Of the forest's ferny floor:
And a bird flew up out of the turret,
  Above the Traveller's head:
And he smote upon the door again a second time;
  'Is there anybody there?' he said.

I repeated the lines now as if they were an unconscious charm directed at Death, the Tempter. I had hardly whispered to myself and to Tiger and to Alice and Miriam when there was the sound of a gunshot. Was it (that gunshot) the cry of the suddenly reawakened drum? Or was it Tiger's shout? Tiger gasped. A hole appeared in his chest into which Death crawled. The blood trickled down and stained his trumpet. He lifted the music of dream-life rebellion, dream-life blood, to his lips and appeared to drink. Well of deprivation. Well of purity. Thus he would slip into popular divinity, popular martyrdom. He spun in the dance. His knees buckled. He clung to a dancing woman in the street and they fell together. In the folklore of the dancing Tiresias Tigers the passage to the underworld is adorned by twining snakes: psychical glass snakes in which are reflected the mystery of the male deprived mask and the mystery of the female deprived mask that Tiresias wears in turn within the logic of the terrible seer.

'O God!' Aunt Miriam cried. 'The police are in the street. And an ambulance driven by Doctor Faustus. The police have been attacked. They have fired at the strikers, Alice.' She stopped and turned to W. H. who advised her on occasions on the direction of her plays. 'May not the shot that kills Tiger signify in our play a prophecy of coming wars, coming battles, in which men, women and children will die?'

'What coming battles?' Alice was sceptical.

Miriam had no reply but I could have written the lines for her: Korea, Vietnam, Cambodia, the Middle East, Nigeria, Uganda, Afghanistan, Tibet, Nicaragua. I could have added, 'Alice thinks it's just a play! Just fiction! Is fiction meant to be real as inner problematic truth, as unpredictable fact, as a blend of the two to stagger our deformities of insight, of perception, of heart and mind?'

Tiger was dead but for a moment it seemed he had not yet breathed his last on 'the crest of a wave' in Miriam's and Alice's little theatre. The ecstasy of purity had cleared his vision for a brief spell. Deprivation of the senses was too *real* to be pure. The villain of the heart was too *real* to be pure white or pure black or pure red. The saint was too real to be divine except when divinity invokes a visionary humanity that sees through the veil of its crimes.

Deprivation was so real it festered into food, deceptive lotus and plague, plenty and poverty.

Hunger was so real that I ascended the moon as if it were Glass in a shoestring ladder and knocked on its door.

'Is there anybody there?' said the Traveller,
  Knocking on the moonlit door.

Belly to belly
Back to back
Ah don't give a damn
Ah done dead a'ready.

And I Tiresias have foresuffered all
I who sat by Thebes below the wall
And walked among the lowest of the dead.

I could not believe it. Ghost was speaking at last. No formal message. A repetition of familiar texts become however strangely cross-cultural, the strangest subversion, where one least suspected or expected to find it in hollow convention or solemn usage. An edge, nothing more, above the malaise, the death-wish of an age: an edge born of temptation that one unravels, perceives, and sifts until it yields a value beyond the immediate taste of temptation, the remorse, the penalty, the rewards.

FIVE

My mother died in 1961. I was sixteen. It was the year the Tiresias Tigers established a new theatre or tent in the magic wood. I heard their muffled drums. Drums swarming with spectres, spectres of the malaise of the twentieth century, a drum upon which the original dancer Tiresias Tiger tapped and tapped and tapped in my dreams. He had arisen from the grave with a hole in his chest when I was three years old.

I played with him (he was a ragged doll) on the drawing-room carpet until he vanished and I did not hear of him, or see him, again until I learnt of the Tiresias Tigers of the magic wood.

Absent or present he was often around the corner in my Sleep and through him I became a pork-knocker scientist who rattled the black hole of gravity in Tiger's chest with a teaspoon.

A frightening eye of sugar or telescopic spoon with which to scrape the barrel of the cosmos, a frightening glimpse into the heart of Ghost. It was also a mystic dream and the beginning of faith. Yes, faith! But faith in what? Was it faith in one's powers to measure prosperity or to be measured by prosperity, to save or to be saved, to know or to be known? Was it faith in heaven or in hell?

A recurring dream that came at least once a year across the waste land of childhood fantasy through the barrel at my gate into quantum quetzalcoatl mathematics in teaspoon and shoe-string middle age.

A disturbing dream for it set into circulation all over again the origins of sensation – such as tasting, rattling silver in a teacup, slicing a bone or a piece of meat that cost a pretty penny.

I know for a fact that an industrial strike over starvation wages occurred on the sugar estates of Old New Forest in 1948 and several strikers were shot dead, one fell in the sugar bowl beneath our window embracing a woman and a child. A tight nightmare fit.

I was three years old when it happened. Three-year-old relic of memory on whose lips was a grain of sugar, on whose lips was a grain of temptation! Memory's repetitive anatomy may lie in a grain of sugar one surreptitiously steals, forbidden sugar, forbidden sweetness! I witnessed the clash with the police from our window above the square. It could have been happening in our drawing room. Alice and Miriam were staring. Staring eyes. Everything and everyone tumbled into a relic of memory as I now write as if I was there yet absent from myself. Absent living body. I saw the hollow ambulance with Doctor Faustus at the skeleton wheel. The commotion of the skeleton bands. BOOM BOOM DOOM DOOM. Commotion, ceaseless sweetness/bitterness elaboration, movement, voices.

Thus I was moved across the years to sift unreliable fact from true play or fantasy and to reconsider the origins of sensation: *an eye in the mouth of a sugar bowl and in the body of Tiresias, the seer.*

Take the seer's eye: in the wake of the shot a *blind* silence enveloped every rattling teaspoon, every gun, every drum, every bone in the crowd in the square beneath our window. Then came an explosion of appetite and anger. I dreamt I saw the dead man move and eat the grain on my lip as he whispered in the hole in his chest, 'Everything you have been tempted to consume recedes into me now, hollow me. See the sweets of violence in dead men's chests, in dead men's lungs, in dead men's hearts, hear the bitterness of explosive suns.

Fifteen suns in a dead man's chest
Yo-ho-ho and the taste of the lotus.

A different bottled ear or eye from the one I received when I reached out to seize the kingdoms of glass, the kingdoms of the globe, and was greeted by my mother's exclamation of joy. An ear and a mouth and an eye in a ragged man's chest . . . I was translated, I was confused, by the telescopic mind of Ghost in Tiger's body.

The drums now spoke to the dead seer, the dead tiger, on the ground.

'Fall down and die, Tiger. We shall pick you up. We shall drum. We shall measure the height of your dance and your fall through ancient Greece and ancient Rome and ancient America and ancient Africa into Robin Redbreast Glass waiting to see old Godot anew. *Old Godot anew, Old Godot anew.* Robin wants to know, wants to see, how far he must fall from the sky into old Godot anew. Why should a beast's sudden death help us to map the ancient heavens anew within the radius of a star, a child's star? One child's star is another's bullet.'

I dreamt I put the question to Ghost and thought I heard him murmur very faintly in the hollow of my ragged doll, 'Life needs death. Life needs death if it is to be. But remember it is *through* death that life measures itself, measures its achievements, its glories. Remember it is *through* death not *with* death – not in league with death as the ultimate violence, the ultimate deprivation. The distinction is a crucial one – it bears on the fabric of the resurrection within every extremity, every hollow . . .' His voice faded. And now it was as if the waiting room of Godot broke its commission with Death and illumined a ragged queue in Tiger's body. Strings were vibrating very subtly, with incredible lightness, incredible *touch* – the sensation of ragged but mysterious alignment with the glories, the achievements, of which Ghost had spoken. I began to marvel across the years and the generations at the sensitivity that lies in the fingers of a ghostly musician touching the leaves of the trees into rhapsodic murmur, the fingers of a ghostly drummer sounding in the Sleep of space, the fingers of green (as they are called) of a ghostly gardener, the fingers of earth of a ghostly man or woman who sculpts a rock and makes it live.

Did I not dream that my own fingers were made of clay – of numb clay – until they scuttled on Glass and became the claws of a bird, then scuttled again, all of a sudden, into an intensity of feeling the instant I cried in my Sleep against the comedian of the machine who would have entrapped me, or seized me, as I alighted on a bell at the end of a rod?

I thought of my grandfather's manuscript (and its ramifications in the simulated world and the real world) – of my mother's staccato fingers drumming on a typewriter as I dreamt I lay within her – of Aunt Miriam's plays revising the histories of the world – and wondered at the origins of perception, the relics of memory that lay as much in me as in ancestral re-visions of *The Waste Land* and of *Faust* in other, nameless, intuitive masterpieces since time began.

I remembered a journey I took when I was five years old through an ancient volume of Sleep. I remembered it all now as I arose from bed and brushed my teeth with the fin of a fish. I remembered my mother who died in 1961. She led me on that journey. She combed my hair with the honeycomb of the sea. She came into my dreams in a long swaying garment made of the sea, and of moss, and of countless stars sprung from the hollow yet resurrected body of Ghost.

Was it a journey into her death or was it a journey we made when I was five years old? *She comes to me when I am old, one hundred years old. The year is 2045. No, not old! Just five, a relic of memory. Five-year-old relic. The year is 1950 on a dusty calendar in an old trunk of books and masks.*

We make our way through the trunk and through the barrel at my gate, the round ship, the round coffin of my ancestors. The year is 1950. I am five years old. My mother gives me a ring. I slip it on to my hand. But as I run on the beach it falls from my finger and is lost forever. Alice is angry. 'You will find it some day,' she says. 'I promise you.' Her voice is sad and angry and I am pierced by foreboding. It was a ring my grandfather had given her. An heirloom or something. Surely she was grossly careless to give it to me before I knew or understood.

Good Ghost! The barrel at our gate was built by me in 1961 a month or two before my mother was drowned. It was built as a memorial to great navigators, great pork-knockers. How could we have made our way through it in 1950 with the lost ring? One is obsessed by time, one is obsessed by the timeless comedy of time. Perhaps the barrel I built in 1961 was invisible to us though it was already there flung up from the bottom of the sea on the crest of a wave of the future as my mother and I stood on the beach facing our grave when I was but a child and she a beautiful, angry woman.

My mother leans on the invisible barrel now.

'It's grandfather's memorial,' I say.

'And the ring?'

'What ring?' I had forgotten.

'A ring of spiritual gold studded with minute diamonds on the inside where it touches your skin. On the inside is the flesh of infancy. On the outside is the wreck of a ship.'

The wreck of a civilization? I was astonished. I lay under the wave of old age and looked up to the sky. I held my five-year-old hand up in the sea to the light of moon-shells, star-shells, sun-shells, and saw for the first time a ring on my mother's skeleton left hand. Had she salvaged it from the sea the day she was drowned? I touched the ring in astonishment. Had I worn it all along and never known it was there?

I touched the ring with the light of my eyes. I felt my mother's lips on my eyes: were they still bitter or were they now sweet?

'If ever you are in trouble,' my mother says – and leans down and lets the sand and the water run through her fingers – 'just brandish it like an asset of state or pawn it for that matter if money's short. Remember it's here to save your life.'

I laughed. Alice laughed. The comedy of an invisible ring, an invisible barrel, an invisible fortune. And yet the tragedy . . . In 1961 when the sea cracked without warning and closed over my mother's hair that fell like lightning to her waist (she was an excellent swimmer and no one at first believed she had drowned) I was left without a blind penny. The house had to be sold to pay off her debts. I remember my Aunt Miriam saying in one of her plays, 'Your mother is extravagant, Robin. Your grandfather left her a treasure. Come and live with me before the world ends.' Was she speaking to me or to W. H.? I went to live with her for a spell on my way to Skull but the house was empty, always empty – she resided now in the waves – and the shadow of W. H. dogged her footsteps as he sought to revive her theatre in the magic wood. They had been close friends, perhaps lovers, and he knew her well. She was sensuous and practical. Sensuous in her deeply grained imagination. Practical in her wit. 'Accept the day-to-day calendar of doom, doom,' she said like a housewife scribbling a list on her pad, 'it's a style the calypso invented for the BBC and all the grand newspapers. They never acknowledge their debt but that's the way of the world, isn't it?' The word *debt* pricked me and I half-awoke to Alice's carelessness and extravagance. Why had I not pawned the invisible ring I wore and raised the money to save our old home from the depredations of strangers?

Too late! Such magical security born of the Ghosts of the sea and the sky comes too late. Too late to save an old house or a lost kingdom.

Lost? Is anything ever absolutely lost? May one not find one's ancestral treasure again by the light, the spirit, the self-mocking humour of vulnerable humanity, self-mocking yet self-revealing visionary touch?

A paradoxical marriage or contract or rehearsal of the origins of tradition runs through all bawdy and sacred generations, the living, the dead, the unborn, to activate the glories of the present and the past and to imply that the body of the resurrection is a medium of ceaseless rapport between original deprivation and original mystery, between newfound being and insensible being, between the tender apparition of hope and derelict, institutional trappings, between past, present and future time and timeless comedies of time.

Between birthday ghosts and old age.

'Come,' Alice and Miriam are saying to me, 'now that you have touched the ring it is time to celebrate your birthday as if it is a royal event. The world shakes with violence. We live in chapels perilous at the bottom of the sea that we must taste like a piece of cake, on the flatlands, in the valleys, on the mountains, on the moon, and in sight of the masquerade of long-haired Halley's comet that we must taste right royally. Here are the origins of the games that children play.'

They hold me and lead me to cosmic theatre in the magic wood. We walk on the crest of the sea and the waves leap and jump and make rain. We are on our way to celebrate my fifth boomsday birthday on a fading dusty calendar. A relic of a newspaper blows at our feet. September 1950 turns to mould in June 1961. The paper twists into spray April 1986 and the apparition of Birthday Ghost. I touch my ring and taste the wreck of civilizations.

164 BC	Birthday Ghost is Babylonian cake.
12 BC	Birthday Ghost is Chinese and Roman cake.
AD 66	Birthday Ghost is broadsword cake over Jerusalem.
AD 295	Birthday Ghost ices the constellation of Andromeda.
AD 451	Birthday Ghost adorns Attila the Hun.
AD 684	Birthday Ghost ices a Nürnberg Tiger.
AD 1066	Birthday Ghost divides William and Harold.
AD 1910	Birthday Ghost submits to photographers.
AD 1985–6	Birthday Ghost dresses up for many a party around the globe.

'Taste it,' said Alice. 'Taste a comet and live. Taste the ridiculous fantasies that are the seed nevertheless of history and tragedy.

Taste illusion. Taste everything that mirrors childhood and old age. Taste until it hurts, it enlightens, it revives a nebulosity of spirit, the nebulous contract with an apparently doomed humanity ingrained into life. That is your royal birthday Robin Redbreast Glass. The merriment of the lost . . . What does it mean?'

I was filled with amazement that such a question had been directed at me. Was I a king or a prince in disguise? Alice seemed so close. Alice, the queen in Miriam's play, is speaking now. She spoke now, she speaks now in a wave, she will speak now in a wave.

'Now is never,' Alice says. 'Now is forever. Now is old age. Now is infancy. Now is Rome. Now is Athens. Now is Babylon. Now is Byzantium. Now is Number Ten. Now is the Kremlin. Now is the White House and a black band playing the blues. Now is the flight of the swallow from summer to winter and back. Now is this precious day in which we live or in which we die.' She is laughing at me. I know she is laughing at me. Alice is laughing at me. And the merry waves jump and subside at our feet under a sea wall.

Her laughter is close and merry, I feel the bite of a wave, I feel bitten by laughter. Does one bite the flesh of a wave when one drowns, when one is borne by the sharp tooth of merriment through death?

What are the origins of such merriment? What are the origins of such bitten/biting laughter, such laughter at death or through death?

It is a game we play in the chapel perilous under the sea at Aunt Miriam's parties. The children dress as rocks, as waves, as moss, as fish, as birds.

I bite into the premises of laughter. I chew the laughing fish and pause in mid-air as if I stand on a balloon in an animal's lung. Boomsday comet or balloon, boomsday lung, boomsday love affair with the pretty girls dressed as fish. Shall I dive into the heart of the balloon and sing, make faces at the chorusing birds? Shall I part my hair behind? Do I dare to eat a peach?

'Come, come Robin,' Aunt Miriam says. 'It's your turn to play. Such a rich costume. Such a glorious balloon.'

I stand awkwardly on the stage. Perhaps I was the envy of the other children. Perhaps – on the other hand – I envied them, I envied the part they were about to play. Aunt Miriam had rigged up a sheet and a blanket as a curtain behind which we stood, Alice and I. Aunt Miriam gave a jerk and the curtain rose like a cloud from the sky. There was a shout and the children swarmed upon us. Fish, animate rocks, birds, animate moss, all came. Indiscriminate laughter. I reached for Alice and she had gone under the wave. I saw her far down in the sea beneath the sheet and the waving blanket, beneath the merry children whose empty graves – untenanted still – are marked with crosses in the sacred wood. I saw the fish dive for her as I dived into my balloon of space. Nothing united us but the tooth of death we shared with all creatures. Nothing now. I nibbled at a bird in the sky. I nibbled at myself. The fish stroked her, the fish stroked itself, the fish stroked Miriam. How sharp, how bitter, is the merry stroke of death at the heart of self-love that cracks at last into the mysterious reflection of others? How sweet, how bitter, is life, the gravity of heart-rending compassion in life? We must laugh with one another or die. We must laugh at our own incompleteness, our grotesqueries, our absurdities, our fallacies, our proneness to despair, our innermost corruption, our innermost violence.

The biter bitten is the tooth of infinite rehearsals of chapels perilous, of the children in Alice's and Miriam's arms under the sea.

Till human voices wake us, and we drown.

SIX

I was wakened by voices I could not fathom. Were they human, were they other than human? I felt an irrational shock that my college education was over. It was a blow. I felt the hollowness of the humanity to which I returned. My mother was an excellent swimmer. Why had she drowned? The afternoon had been blissful. She had taken our boat *Tiger* to sea and we were drifting lazily a mile or two off the coast. Such trips were not unusual. This was the third excursion in June 1961. Aunt Miriam was there. Five children were there including Peter and Emma, two close friends of my own age, orphaned in early childhood, who lived with Alice and me. I was there. (No! I am confused. I would have been there but was down with flu and lay in bed at Aunt Miriam's. W. H. insists that it was *he* who lay in bed with flu and has another tale to tell that I shall disclose in due course.)

From my bed in Miriam's house I could see the sky and the sea. I could see Peter and Emma whose lives my mother saved. It was they who brought the news to me, messengers of the roaring laughter of the deep through which they came. I could see the wall and the floor and the window that Miriam used as a stage from which to launch her chapel perilous plays in which I had participated, forever participated, even before I was born, or time appeared to begin.

The blanket and the sheet she erected as a curtain were now missing. Yet they lay on me. I was in them. I was in the sea. I was their being of Sleep. I was the absent players, absent body yet present relic of memory. Sleepwalking relic on a wave of Sleep where my mother played a role that was to recur again and again within my dreams. Dream chapel perilous under the sea as a prelude to chapel perilous of the flatlands, chapel perilous Skull, chapel perilous of the Mountain of Folly, chapel perilous of space.

The boat sailed across the floor. *It cracked.* Was it a fist of wind shaking the house? Was it the floor that heaved, was it the boat? One of those unexpected tremors or earthquakes that shook the magic wood across the years. Just a tremor but it drove the boat upon the reef.

Fever inflates one's perceptions of things. High fever. My finger grew large (or was it small) as a tooth clawing at a rock. My lung ballooned and I dived at a bird skimming a wave. The weather suddenly changed. The window on the stage shook. *Tiger* overturned into a ragged chest, ragged inner sail, inner curtain, ragged cross-currents. Alice bobbed up in Tiger's tail and swam with Peter and Emma to land. She swung back and dived through grandfather's ring to save the others. It was the last I saw of her from my wave of Sleep. I held her close. She fell into the Glass of time. Timelessness.

Within a year I packed a ghostly pork-knocker bag, secured a spiritual compass, sharpened my drowned ghost-pen, and set out into the sacred wood to make my way in the world, the hollow world, and in the multi-textual regions of space.

The old house in which Alice, Peter, Emma and I had lived belonged now to strangers. Before I left I scouted in a cellar in Miriam's playhouse and little theatre (occupied now by W. H.) and unearthed a trunk of masks from Tiger's bobbing chest on a wave of Sleep.

I recalled our last New Year's Eve party (celebrated in Hogmanay style), my echoing voice in Miriam's at midnight.

We twa hae paddl'd in the burn
  Frae morning sun till dine,
But seas between us braid hae roared
  Sin' auld lang syne.

'Where is laughter?' I asked Aunt Miriam. 'Laughter's mask?' but she hid her face in the seas. I saw her tears despite the running waters but these too were woven into another mask in Tiger's broken body. I left it there out of tenderness and respect. At the bottom of an old man's cargo of dreams when he revisits the past.

My eye fell on another mask on which W. H.'s shadow fell and this I pulled from the trunk. Shadow and substance. It imbued me with a sensation of renewed inner substance, inner fictional being.

'I am a stranger,' I said to the mask of Shadow and Substance in which I was reflected even as I reflected it.

'Why a stranger?'

I looked at it closely. It was indeed a mask that I knew as if from a great distance. I knew I would come to inhabit it in the future as ageing fictional author in fictional youth, fictional character mirroring and mirrored by transformative relics of memory. It was the mask in which I would write my life, my fictional autobiography.

It was adorned by the tooth I had seen in the chapel of the sea, the tooth I shared with all creatures, a tooth sharper than any pen that I would come to possess. It had eaten its lines, its poetries, its scripts, into the flesh of my spirit. It had cut a long ravine along my brow. It had cut chasms and gulfs. It had shaped my mouth, my lips, to register the miracle of innermost address, innermost self-judgement. It was the tooth of judgement day, ceaseless judgement day I both longed for and dreaded.

'I am a stranger to you,' I said to the mask. 'I reflect you and that is all. I wander the highways and byways of time in search of a gesture that rejects you entirely. I loathe you. I loathe the future. I want to be eternally young, eternally strong.'

'Can you reject the future?' the mask replied. 'Even the dead must reckon with the future if there is to be justice, justice for the unborn son, the unborn daughter, the unborn stranger. You call yourself a stranger! Even the dead . . . Much more so the stranger who comes from the dead, dead fictions, dead legacies, dead traditions, that are not as dead as they seem but *alive*, alive as a threat or a challenge we have not yet absorbed, alive as revisionary fabric, revisionary truth.'

The mask paused but continued before I could speak: 'I am the future in which you will write of this moment, this present moment, and of the past. I am you when this century draws to a close. I am you in the twenty-first century. I am the memory of the future. You are fortunate, Robin Glass.'

'How so?' I demanded. 'I am a stranger. Of that I am sure.'

'A fortunate stranger,' said the mask. 'To speak through the stranger in yourself means this: you are actually *in* the present moment and yet *outside of/beyond* the present moment by a fraction – shall I say – by an edge . . . But that is enough to be *in* the world yet to move by a fraction above the chaos of the world; it is – let me put it this way – to see yourself in an infinite body lying still with Alice and Miriam and the other children in the sea yet, at liberty, by a hair's breadth to approach yourself as in a play, relate to yourself in the memory of the future, be in yourself yet move – as I have said – just a fraction beyond a stranger's death, out of *your* stillness, *your* death. One day you will come upon Peter and Emma in the stranger city of Skull that stands upon a simulated arch or bridge between true voice and true ear, true response to the everlasting intimate stranger in yourself.

'Ah Stranger! you move within yet without yourself. You dream in every age of the womb from which you came as if the womb were a theatre of existence and you are steeped in it even as you surface from it or fall to the edge of time, *visionary* backwards fall, *visionary* downwards fall, *visionary* upwards fall, *visionary* forwards fall. To transform the vertigo of a stranger birth, a stranger death, in yourself is to fall into the resurrectionary/revolutionary Glass of your age . . .'

Ghost's voice faded. For it was Ghost I suddenly saw masquerading as my future self.

I looked at Ghost and knew, despite everything he had said, I loathed his appearance, his sagging cheeks, his age, his apparitional freedom. Yes *freedom*! One is afraid of the coming of old age because one hates one's stranger capacity for freedom, for spiritual justice through and beyond one's trappings, cultural trappings, etc. One dreads the heartrending call of supreme insight, the pain and the anguish of stranger maturity, the slow but inevitable dissolution of the ego, the dissolution of the proud but unfree state or body in its tantrums and rages and incurable desires. One dreads a true marriage with the stranger beloved in all creation – a beloved creation one may learn to touch anew, to sense anew, to know anew beyond all self-deception or arrogance. A beloved creation that astonishes, disturbs: it brings a mirror into the heart of creaturely terror and addictive lust. It asserts anew within the perversities of ambition a necessary quest for the foundations of religious hope where one least suspects these to exist. For some unaccountable reason I thought of poor Emma and Peter. What had they made of their lives, of their survival? Would they disturb me profoundly (yet illumine my quest for religious hope) when I came upon them in the city of Skull?

One is afraid to drown before one's time (yet live), one is afraid to glimpse the age of the earth (yet descend into the womb), the age of faltering economies (yet arise into the spirit of value), the age of the tides, the age of ageless fall into apparent nothingness . . . all before one's time . . . the age of terrifying responsibility, the necessity to create a true and intimate life of conscience, life of authority within the body of the waste land.

TOWARDS DROWNED SUNRISE IN JUNE 1962 – A YEAR AFTER *TIGER* STRUCK THE REEF AND BROKE – I (ROBIN REDBREAST GLASS) CAME TO THE EDGE OF A BLACK SWAMP OR LAKE, THE EDGE OF THE CHAPEL PERILOUS OF THE FLATLANDS. The chapel or city (it had not yet been transformed into a wealthy city) was called SKULL. It stood above an ancient sea-bed. The ocean had rolled here long, long ago on its way to the foot of the Angel Falls escarpment in the magic wood. Boomsday Skull. Boomsday Tiger. I stared into the mirror of the swamp and saw Skull's future, its lavish prosperity. I heard the voice of Ghost nevertheless. 'I am in all decrepit humanity. I am in the broken Tiger. I am in the sad dancers who ride on the waves. I am in all lost loves and lost lovers. I am ghost within ghost within ghost.' I saw my reflection in a ghostly wave, my seventeen-year-old drowned reflection in the water, half-in the sleeping tides that pillowed my eyes, half-out yet in the biting mask of Ghost, half-in my seventeen-year-old shredded skeleton – dressed to look beautiful now, immortal now, in the theatre of Faustian history – half-out yet in the memory bank of the future and in the ageing global mask that Ghost had employed as *me* in the 1980s and the 1990s and in the year 2000 when Skull would have achieved the status of a faeryland Chernobyl tomb, cheap electricity and deceptively abundant goods.

'Why me?' I cried. 'Why choose *me*? Who is it – let us be truthful, Ghost – that writes of *me* as if he is *me* in the future? Some damned expert no doubt. (They have ruined the water table in many a flatland, they have despoiled and exploited resources, triggered erosion in global theatres – experts they call themselves, experts in everything *cheap* though God knows how dear one's embalmed species may ultimately prove.) Did I not happily drown when Alice and Miriam drowned? Whose body of expertise am I? Whose dear poverty, whose cheap prosperity, am I?'

I uttered the questions without thinking. I spoke, it seemed, in a dream without knowing I had spoken. I was alive yet dead. Why had I spoken as I had? Dream-reflex? Skull-protest? Simulated freedom of speech? Such speech (such uncertainty of motivation) sprang out of a fear, an ambivalence, a distrust of futures that come upon one before one knows the choices one is making, before one knows one's potential age, one's deepest age, one's cross-cultural heritage and body of wisdom to come abreast of the tools that may damn or save (one cannot say) the human race.

Such involuntary speech (half-simulated, half-unscripted) sprang out of the dilemmas of a post-colonial civilization, out of Third Worlds, and bewildered First Worlds. Out of ancient conquests and legacies of evil that Alice and Miriam and all the Calypsonians had danced and played in all apparent and perverse innocence.

I repeated my questions and added automatically, 'Can one trust the experts who write the fictions of the future?'

Ghost hid his Birthday/Deathday humours in a cloud then spoke above the chapel of the flatlands. 'I shall call upon W. H. in a moment or two to speak of the book of your life. No expert is he but an adversary.'

'Adversary!' I exclaimed.

'Are the truths of fiction,' said Ghost, 'not rooted in an adversarial spirit? Take the fictional houses of God! We call them cathedrals. Admirals and generals and soldiers everywhere. And the saints. Where are they? In a stained-glass window or two where they resist oblivion.' Ghost was jesting but I experienced a stab of fear. 'Perhaps W. H. will elbow me . . .'

'And you will elbow him,' Ghost interrupted, 'into revisionary strategies in which *you* live as if your hand, your being, your touch, your seeing, your hatreds and fears for that matter, your innermost fantasies, become a medium in which life and death wrestle with one another.'

'What are revisionary strategies?' I was uncertain.

'I say revisionary strategies to imply that as you write of other persons, of the dead or the unborn, bits of the world's turbulent, universal unconscious embed themselves in your book. Do you see?'

'And I revise around these and through these. I see.' I was filled with a sudden animosity towards W. H. 'It is *my* life – not W. H.'s. I shall spit in his eye when we next meet for a rehearsal at Aunt Miriam's in her chapel perilous play of the flatlands.'

Ghost was laughing soundlessly. 'Did not Christ heal a blind man with spittle and clay? It's an elaborate strategy simple as it appears. In your case, Robin, it implies that your backward fall into Miriam's childhood theatre is the visionary substance and the bitter *flavour* of memory, a relic of memory on your tongue that fills you with such uneasiness you project it upon W. H. And in so doing you help him to *see* deeper into the fabric of intuitive theatres, theatres of clay as of sea, light and darkness, air and element, theatres of the past, theatres of the present, theatres of the future.'

I was struck by the parallels Ghost had drawn.

'*Intuitive* theatres?'

'Just so,' said Ghost. 'They illumine the blind life (the unconscious bits) of the imagination whose roots run deep into the diverse substance of the intimate stranger in yourself Robin Glass, the clay, the claws, and everything that translates into innermost perception. The truths of fiction, yes! They validate you. You are the substance of stranger quarrels – love's quarrel with time is a healed passageway into God – stranger myth, untameable reality, and renaissance of faculties within the womb of space. You *live* and write your fictional autobiography from the other side of W. H.'s blind/seeing mind, Robin Glass. He is a character in your book. You are no invention of his. You are no pawn of his. You validate and contest his discoveries. They are your discoveries as much as his.' Ghost was laughing but deadly serious. 'I merely confer upon him a body and a mask that are an extension of my paradoxical Being and of your youth into fictional middle and old age in which you lift your pen and write as you now do of your adversary W. H.'

I was conscious suddenly of W. H.'s presence and mask in my book.

'May I give you the facts?' said W. H. 'I may be a character in your book but still . . .'

'Facts?' said I.

'You – Robin Glass – your mother Alice, your aunt Miriam, and three children were drowned in June 1961, the afternoon of the earthquake. The boat *Tiger* overturned at sea. Alice, brave woman, assisted Peter and Emma, helped them to the land and returned.'

My hatred of W. H. welled into fury. 'It's not true,' I shouted. 'You know damn well I was in bed with flu at Aunt Miriam's.'

'It was I,' said W. H. gently.

'*You*?'

'Shadow and substance ail everywhere in adversarial contexts of history. And out of that illness is born the resurrection of the body of the soul that we share with one another, black with white, humanity with humanity. What more can you ask of me, Robin Glass, what greater quest, what greater truth? We share an enduring tradition.'

'You spoke of facts,' I insisted.

'Facts, yes, in that fate is the mask authorial freedom wears – the fate of a realistic end or extermination – until it yields to true myth we share with one another, the future with the past. When I arose from bed on hearing news of your death my illness vanished. I knew that time itself had changed and I had become the character of true myth in your book. Not that I was surprised. I had been rehearsing the part for a long time. I had been your aunt's lover (I had grown to care for you as if you were my nephew) and the producer, the director, of her plays – a background figure. Background yet close as a shadow is to its substance. (Are not authors – forgive me for calling myself an author in this instance – shadow relatives in the book of life? And thus as shadows indispensable to the body of life, the fiction of the body?) When I heard the news I ran, ill as I was, healed nevertheless, blind, seeing nevertheless, down to the sea. The waves were high. The reef – a mile or so away – was a mass of turbulent ocean. A terrible commotion of water. Emma and Peter had already been taken away. It was rumoured your mother Alice swam ashore with them and returned for Miriam and the others. *I thought I heard a voice from the ocean cry*: "Remember me as I remember you. Become a character in my book. Fiction is real when authors become unreal. Fiction reveals its truths, its genuine truths that bear on the reality of persons, the reality of the world, when fiction fictionalizes authors and characters alike. Thus is archetypal myth resurrected. Thus am I your nephew if not in blood in the language we share."

'The voice in the ocean ceased,' said W. H., 'and yet I had been so stirred that a crowd seemed to flock out of the waves into my heart and mind. "Fiction relates to presences and to absences," they said. "Fiction gives buoyancy to us. Fiction explores the partiality of the conditioned mind and the chained body, chained to lust, chained to waste. Fiction's truths are sprung from mind in its illumination of the sensible body again and again and again, in its illumination of our grasp of intuitive theatre and of deprivation in the materials with which one constructs every quantum leap from the sick bed of humanity." ' The crowd of voices subsided and W. H.'s confession faded into the page on which I wrote. I moved along the edge of the swamp to the Skull-shaped simulated city of the flatlands. And experienced the oddest vertigo – the vertigo of one's precipitous age, the heady manifestos, the ambitions, the ideal fallacies, the intoxications, the addictions, the heights – though walking on the flatlands! I – Robin Glass – should have 'walked tall' as the President of the United States or as the Chairman of the Soviet Union but sagged instead (when no one was looking). Was it a necessary terror of the resurrection to experience oneself as a young man in a hollow body? Hollow-looking glass marvel in every television box! Such is the illusion of power the resurrected body faces as it ascends from the grave. It is encrusted with illusions of power, illusions of freedom, that it needs to unravel as a prelude to a genuine revolution.

I loathed Ghost as if he had occasioned the vertigo of my arousal. My loathing had intensified when he began to speak a variety of uncomfortable home truths. 'Better a dumb Spirit than a speaking God. Such are the paradoxes born of the Word and of the possession of a voice by a stranger exercised in true capacity or spiritual right.'

Ghost had made an enemy of me by speaking the language of the judging heart. God had made an enemy of Mankind with every commandment that he uttered. The earth became a battlefield of fanaticisms, one party fighting another, each defending but attacking God in mauling the stranger at the gate. Each was convinced it possessed a duty to maim or to kill in upholding the laws of God. Such is the terror and the ambiguity of the Word. No wonder God tended to keep a silent tongue in His head. Or was it in Her head? (The matter of gender was a sore point amongst male priests and female priests.) Ghost had ventured to speak through a variety of masquerades and utterances that seemed to mock yet to reveal, to discount yet to make visible innermost feuding reality that is masked by self-righteous accent or idiom, self-righteous deprivation.

Indeed this was Ghost's strategy on behalf of a lost or half-remembered humanity on the edge of the abyss, on the edge of hollow intelligences, hollow prides, into which I moved as resurrected flesh-and-blood within the age of the waste land.

It was this uncertainty about the Word, about truth, in my resurrected body invoking the half-remembered shell I once was that tormented me most of all in returning to the land from the sea and intensified once again my indictment of Ghost. Was I now *more* than human shell, *less* than human hollow, *other* than human shell, in tending to forget (within the grave from which I had arisen) an everlasting strangeness in creaturely divinity's essence, an everlasting saturation of fabric and necessity for a spiritual irony in all renascent formations, animal and soul, angel and fish and bird?

Was this spiritual irony part and parcel of the seed of Ghost in the Word of God?

Did that seed in its grain of self-mockery and profoundest utterance sustain a true placelessness, a true freedom on land and water and air (*not* a technological roar or self-righteous bias), profoundest change, profoundest imagination (*not* ten feet tall cliché-ridden idols and derivatives of global conquest)?

I saw it all now with heartrending insight and remorse such as only the dead who return to the living may know. I had come back from the chapel of the sea with Ghost long, long ago. In dreaming of him on the beach I had been involved in a rehearsal of perfectible order, perfectible industry, perfectible state, that I shared with him from the beginning of time. But in my obliviousness of the ambiguity of the Word and the nature of absence that the dead endure (absence from a hollow humanity) and absence's ramifications in native presence, I had had to dream again and again of obsessional need, obsessional wealth, obsessional poverty, obsessional expectation of a supreme prosperity as if prosperity were its own perfectible Ghost, perfectible commander of the futures of the race.

'Supreme prosperity?' Ghost said to me now from within the

masquerades of dream. 'Supreme irony! The perfectibility of the state, the perfectibility of command, the perfectibility of industry, leads to a growing tide of refugees of spirit in flight from themselves to an illusory benefactor. And your resurrection – each rehearsal in which I am involved with you – is as much a warning of the sickness of the expectant soul as it is a vision of a divine and terrifying love. My fear is, Robin, that the sickness of expectant souls may prevail for a long, long time to come (with increasingly dangerous consequences) in a disordered and chaotic world in flight to a prosperity it confuses with the genius of love. But then have we not sown obsessional desire, obsessional folly, in the waste land that we cherish?'

I thought I had sown the origins of sensation, dance, touch, flowering of poetry . . . Yes, I thought I had sown such occasions in my library of dreams but everything seemed hollow now. I strove to articulate that hollowness into the 'withinness' of the Word, a 'withinness' that was transformative wholeness in the vessel of space, the hollow vessel of space; and failed. I sought to articulate that hollowness into the 'withoutness' of Spirit, Spirit that immerses itself in the fabric of being yet moves at the edge of the fury of hypocritical slogan and quarrelsome rhetoric upon a plane of reality; and failed. But in failing I knew that that hollowness was the ground of creative conscience and value, the ground of an absence from the world that re-enters the world without illusion, without ideal self-deception. Did the absent body – in re-entering the theatre of the world – begin to acquire its own true echoing voice in a hollow humanity whose hollowness became an unsuspected creative faculty in the vitalized conscience of tradition, the vitalized conscience of the dead?

Did the absent body – in re-entering the theatre of the world as resurrected presence – begin to acquire a capacity to dislodge prepossession and formidable bias within a hollowness of humanity whose conscription of value inevitably shifts or cracks or moves before the breath of Spirit?

One cannot return from the dead, return to the present, without sensing in some degree – however ambiguously – through failure or achievement – that the miracle of a re-entry into a hollow humanity is a subversive reality one has neglected to explore in its ramifications within the origins of value.

I had come to the bridge of wisdom. It arched across the flatlands and across the swamp of adventure through which Raleigh and Cortes and Middle Passage Rastafarian Magellan and many others had moved to the block or the fire or to the grave. Were they in essence refugees of spirit bound together in the chaos of the world? Black refugees. White refugees. Conquistadorial adventurers and refugees. Victimized emigrants or immigrants or refugees. No wonder W. H. had heard such a clamour in the sea whose voices he barely caught and faintly translated.

The bridge was a simulated arch in my Faustian dream of Third Worlds running hand in hand with First or Second Worlds. It stretched between the true (however faint) voice of the absent body and the true (however remote) ear of the absent body, the true voice *in* and the intimate response *from* the everlasting stranger in oneself.

I was greeted by an illumination that seemed nevertheless fraught with danger: the *cheap* light of the sun, the *cheap* light of a furnace, in a drowned man's refugee eyes as he arises from the chapel perilous of the sea and is tempted by Prosperity Ghost in the city of Skull.

How cheap is the light of the sun, how cheap is the electricity of the stars?

'Cheapness is all,' said Ghost. But I saw that his eyes were sad. Intimate, knowing, sad eyes within the everlasting stranger in oneself. 'Cheapness is all,' the refugees roared and would have rushed into Skull but their way was barred as if Time itself were considering their plight before it yielded to their demand.

'Why should Time yield to such temptation?' I said to Ghost. 'You should know since you raise the issue in this masquerade . . .'

'Prosperity Ghost you mean!' he was laughing soundlessly.

'Yes! Indeed. You raise the issue in this masquerade as a moral aesthetic, I take it – a piece of moral theatre. Miriam loved moral theatre! And I – resurrected bone and flesh that I am – cannot shake it out of my veins. Hollow veins in which I taste nevertheless an impulse to regenerative vessel, regenerative capacity. And so I ask as if the tooth I bring from the grave *bites* so fiendishly, so terribly, I cannot resist asking (I cannot resist hunting the truth): would it not be kinder, much kinder, of Time to resist the will of the hordes who rush into the lap of exploiters and into the arms of illusory benefactors? Would it not be kinder, much kinder, of Time to assist the growing tide of refugees to draw closer to their innermost conscience, to resist the cheap and the tawdry, to resist the ruthless calculation, the ruthless, the unprincipled?'

'Time yields,' said Ghost so softly I could scarcely hear (I held my resurrected ear now to the deck of the Faustian bridge to catch the true and bitter voice of hollow self, the true and bitter response to hollow self) 'because it is endemic part and parcel of the fodder of generations. Time is *not* love, divine love. Time is a character of universality incorrigibly stained by partial, biased and cruel forces. Because of its partiality its biases are susceptible to excavation and to the true action of redemptive love, redemptive wholeness. But that is another matter. A matter for the creative and aroused conscience within the graves of history. In regard to your immediate question that bears on the logic of time, Time as an answering device, a speaking device, a machine in the chaotic soul, Time (note I sometimes spell it with a common t, sometimes a capital T) is but a measure of partial events.

'Look! Look into the swamp of the centuries within your own book that is stained by invisible creek water, invisible river water, invisible pork-knocker barrels, pork-knocker ships; just look! What do you see?'

Before I could answer – as if I were an answering clock – Ghost continued: 'You see when you scan closely your own death and the deaths of your mother and aunt (whose antecedents came into the magic wood from other continents) that the refugee count in the clock of the sea has moved from adventurers and slaves, from those who fled the sword and the fire, from those who stood on the auction block, into disrupted twentieth-century populations broken by famine or civil war; tyrannized by military regimes; deceived by politicians who rig the ballot when there are elections in the Third World.

'Their lust for prosperity and their despair are such (and who amongst us can blame them?) that they turn from the brutalities of the sovereign state and the phoney placards of newfound independence and fall on their knees before the new El Dorados of the West.'

'New El Dorados?' I was sceptical. 'There is growing unemployment. There is the rise of labour-saving devices, new clocks whose every tick manufactures redundancy. And this is Skull. It is the archetypal Colony in the magic wood. It stands in or over a swamp.'

'The archetypal Colony may seem remote from the West but it is an extension of the West. The refugees will come. Indeed they have never ceased to come, sometimes as a trickle, sometimes as a wave. Look deep! Look deep into the heart of the swamp that stains every page of history. Look deep into the necessity to manufacture asylums for refugees, ghetto asylums, god knows what. Scrap a couple of rockets, a couple of nuclear bombs, half a dozen submarines and battleships, an extra penny or two on income tax, and heigho, Skull may be converted into a prosperous concentration camp.

'Think of the prospect of cheap energy. Look deep, I say, into the swamp. Look deep into the cheap electric stars and the cheap electric suns reflected there in the mirror of coming technologies, coming at any price, any human price. Look into the brave new world. Look into the faeryland promise of Chernobyl. Time lifts its skirt like a radioactive whore.'

All my ancient and modern loathing or detestation of Ghost returned. 'This is a joke, an obscene joke,' I cried. 'Face the facts. Don't exaggerate. Chernobyl is a disaster complex in the Soviet Union. What has it got to do with the free West and the choices that lie before the electorates of the free West? Are you saying such choices are an illusion?' I felt the shadow of terror in my resurrected body. 'What bearing has faeryland on Skull?'

'Hush-hush disaster, dateless day bearing,' said Ghost. 'When Communist Rome burns an empire of souls inhales its ash. But no one sees the fire or the brute faery at the extremities of our fingertips. So too when faeryland burns (and the absent body you wear and loathe and which you and I share, as a multi-faceted investiture with which to address and warn the world, looms into theatre) the building blocks of heaven are shaken by the storm. But no one sees or hears the earthquake – not even those who are experimenting with human souls. Skull, dear Robin Glass, is our coming asylum for the refugee spirit. Skull is the dateless day that Faust simulates. Skull is the transformation of the swamp of history into an electric paradise. Cheap energy is the opium of the masses, the new lotus.'

I felt the hordes of the future rush through me into Skull. I pencilled some notes into my book.

Dateless Day Play. Dateless Day (plucked from a pre-Columbian infinity calendar) relics of memory. Hollow humanity.

Tooth and ring. Chapel perilous of the sea (AD 1961–2).

Bridge into Skull. Chapel perilous of the flatlands (AD 1962).

Indistinct clamour of refugees of spirit. Cheap energy is all (AD 1962–86).

Faeryland burns at Chernobyl (AD 1986).

Capital investment for Play of Humanity begins in Skull. Asylum for refugees. Marvellous glittering tomb-shaped edifice. Twenty-first century sophisticated concentration camp. Fodder of generations (AD 2000–2050).

I re-read my notes. My loathing of Ghost intensified. I tore the notes into scraps but they floated over the water like a measure of the dancing city, the dancing theatre, of Skull.

Towers were built. Promenades. Halls. Shopping precincts. Streets. Etc., etc., etc. It was a grand play, a grand village. One matter had been omitted from my notes. And now I found myself pencilling it with invisible lead on to the brow of Skull.

Plutonium has been found. Sophisticated Third World/First World dump in the text of the magic wood.

I tried to tear this up too but the bone in the masks of Skull that some of the players wore in the Play of Humanity resisted my touch.

Yet the sensation reminded me of the enigma of time, time's bone as well as time's page, and I found myself tracing a calendrical road that ran into the theatre of Skull. It was called Dateless Day Infinity Route or Tunnel. I moved along it to its junction with Prospero Mall. And here it was that I came upon Peter and Emma in the year AD 2025. Was this an arbitrary calendrical year or was it a provocative and lucid dream-choice reflecting the measureless yet ironically pinpointed canvas in the drama of the future within the life of the creative present?

I reached out to them from within the tunnel: I back from the drowned dead in each year, each century; they hovering still, it seemed, at the margins of the pinpointed living where the spray of the sea in every leaf, in every flower, broke our lips into a kiss.

Tunnel of immortality? Tunnel of death? Tunnel of the resurrection?

As our hands and lips met and parted I felt I had aged not a whit since AD 1962. Peter and Emma, on the other hand, were my own age yet they seemed older than I in the tunnel or the relic or the passageway of memory in which we stood. Was it ten years older? Was it twenty years older? I puzzled over the difference. What is five years or ten years or twenty years between friends? And yet – since Peter and Emma and I were actually the same age – it became important to know why they seemed older, I younger, why in another light of dream-theatre I might become older, they younger. Were such values of time purely arbitrary, purely conventional aspects of story line in the play of a civilization? Or were they a reflection of absent bodies entering time, excavating time, changing our innermost grasp of fate and of freedom within the veil of time?

I knew it all signified a measure of ironic spirituality and dream-choice in the way one excavates the biases of time, the tyrannies of time. Each relic of time, each built passageway, each sculpted tunnel or bowl or room, each cell, each cradle, glimmered with the cruelties of the past yet with a theatre of new-born spirit to breach or transform a moment of terror.

Each minute distinction of years between me and Peter and Emma in the theatre of spirit reflected our vision or capacity to see or feel or grasp the urgencies and the consequences in the architectures and connective rooms of our age. And in opening a dream-tunnel that ran from the middle of the twentieth century into the twenty-first century we were involved not only in generations but in the pinpointed canvas of the years, in one's illusory yet immortal youth as much as in one's illusory and immortal old age.

One was involved in the nature and the meaning of survival as much as in unravelling a distinction in minute accretions in the value of time within childhood theatre, within resurrectionary theatre, within political theatre.

I knew there was a distinction between simulated immortality or youth or old age and the terrifying insights associated with a resurrection/a revolution of inner mind, inner spirit.

In this instance – in reaching out to Emma and Peter – I was assailed by the enigma of authorship and charactership across the years in the Play of Humanity and in my fictional autobiography.

One loomed large (the play of humanity) whereas the other, my book, was minute but intensely real, intensely poignant.

In AD 1962 – when I came within hailing distance of Skull – I was aware of Ghost's extension of himself into W. H.'s ageing mask through which I wrote my fictional autobiography.

Now, however – in AD 2025 – though I remained as young as ever (my hair was immaculately black and I was dressed to a *t* or a *T* in the paradox of time/Time) I knew that W. H. himself had vanished and that someone else – some other ageing mask – played the role of authorship/charactership in my book as if I were he, he me. The name or the initials on this new ageing mask eluded me. Yet they marked a further and crucial development in my book. They implied the secretion of ageless myth in the theatre of the world as a subtle rebuttal of an authoritarian realism – however sophisticated – an authoritarian story line or sophisticated dumping ground in the theatre of Skull for an irrelevant and a doomed humanity held in thrall by the logic of violence, the logic of hell. In that subtle rebuttal lay the foundations of religious hope. But even so I could not be sure how precarious such foundations were, how costly they might prove. How possible, or impossible, it was to make a beginning – nothing more – in switching the priorities of Billionaire Death away from the cinematic dance and extermination of the brutes (that claimed the bright lights of Broadway Skull) into scenarios of a hospital of infinity at the heart of space.

Perhaps Peter and Emma knew of such beginnings and might be able to disclose some unsuspected shift in the priorities of Skull. For they (Peter and Emma) were themselves characters of myth. They had become this in peculiar, uncertain and groping – even self-contradictory – degrees in the midst of the desolations of Prosperity. One finds such characters in every city, in every throng of refugees. The odd survivors. They belong yet do not belong. In some quite lucid and strangely factual way I knew I existed in their dreams – that they were dreaming of me as I dreamt of them at a junction in the tunnel where the resurrection of the dead seemed to blend with the survival of the endangered living.

I knew that their dreams of me were intensely real, that their survival, their escape from drowning, had so affected them, that I was in the very fibre of their lives, an eternal question mark, an eternal misgiving. I was the seed of their terror and their uncertainty in Skull. What did survival truly mean when all those who are dearest to one have vanished? Equally they were for me the seed of religious hope. What did resurrection/revolution truly mean unless one could place it in living, uncertain flesh-and-blood within oneself/without oneself?

'I have been looking for you for ages,' I said to them. 'And now at last . . .' I hesitated but rushed on. 'The resurrection's a fact, Emma. It's no panacea, Peter. It doesn't stop the pain of living. That I now know. I can tell you this. If anything it intensifies mental anguish. For one sees into the shell of what one was. One sees into the bankruptcy of one's civilization: a terrible business. And yet one loves one's fellow woman and man as never before. One truly knows the fabric of compassion, of pity, of beauty. A terrifying kind of longing, of hope, within the hollowness of one's age.'

Peter was staring hard at me. 'That's why I became an addict,' he said. 'Self-love. Egotistical love. Break all sound barriers. I drink the lotus, the opium of the masses. The death wish of an age. I am a popular singer and player and I feed on the lotus, belly to belly, back to back death wish in Calypso's and Tiger's band. A new lament, a new ballad of the soul, Robin!' He was staring at me quizzically and I could not be sure how serious he was, whether he was testing me, mocking me, mocking himself, testing himself.

Emma tore the shred of incipient but mutual addiction, mutual self-pity from our eyes. 'That's not what Robin is saying, Peter,' she said to me as though she were addressing him. Her voice softened. 'Poor Peter! He's an incurable romantic, Robin. But what would I do without him? Robin's talking of a voice and an ear, Peter, we seldom hear or use. Not BOOM, BOOM, DOOM, DOOM. He's saying it's a voice and an ear we *may* come to perceive within ourselves when we return to ourselves and know ourselves for the first bleak and terrible time. Without fallacy. Without illusion. Nothing egotistical. Know suddenly at the heart of despair the true stranger in ourselves, Peter, beyond all our vanity in whom lies the promise of glory.'

She uttered the word 'glory' with reluctance, misgiving. An abused word. Napoleonic glory? The glory of lust? I knew she meant neither of these. What did she mean? It was as if she had read the question in my mind as I had read the question in hers in the tunnel of classical penetration, classical endurance, classical genius of love. *I saw in a flash that she was a priest*, a female priest, she was hope in the city of Skull, revolutionary hope, unconventional hope.

'It's divine Communism,' Peter murmured, 'when the male priest sups with the female priest at the same high table in the tunnel of centuries . . .' He stopped as if he had said too much. But even so it was a definition of 'divine' and of 'Communism' I had never heard before. Still I wondered. What was 'divine Communism'? Like 'glory' it was of debased coinage, an abused term. Take 'Communism'! What was 'Communism'? Surely not the Communist Rome that burnt at Chernobyl while the Party fiddled. Take 'divine'! What was the 'divine'? Surely not the pomp and the robes in the theatre of Skull.

Emma, the priest, caught the drift of reflection. She turned to Peter as if he were me in the veil of the tunnel and I were he in the play of divinity. 'When one breaks true bread,' she said, 'with the true stranger in oneself who knows one, is unsparing with one, yet perceives the creative conscience and potential in one, then one begins an ascent through the follies of one's age to a vision of divine Communism. Alas it's not easy.' Her eyes were both dark and pale. I saw she wished to goad me, to startle me, within our pattern of lucid dream. She shot at me, 'You, Robin, will need Peter as *alter ego* stranger – *alter ego* theatre – when you climb the Mountain of Folly above Skull.'

A beam shone through the tunnel that alerted us – Peter, Emma and I – to dateless day infinity comedy in which we were involved. Perhaps it was Emma's allusion to '*alter ego* theatre' that reminded me of the ruses and the labyrinths of *Faust*, the simulated voices, simulated scripts, that passed as normality in Skull. Imagine the various factories, pubs, bedrooms, drawing rooms, football arenas, offices, stages – imagine the elegant and violent puppetries, the strings that are pulled, the solemn manifestos, the rages, the brutalities, the sermons, the curses, the drunken fights, the programmes, the dangling shadow of bait – imagine the follies of which Emma had spoken. Follies of Skull! Circus of Skull! Reflexes of Skull!

We – Emma, Peter and I – were caught in the web of Skull reflexes and automatic behaviours that passed for normality. And yet . . . I paused, reflected again. Did I mean *abnormality*? There lay a distinction between ourselves and the 'normal' world. We accepted our abnormality and the bizarre truths associated with ourselves as a capacity to mirror yet repudiate and breach Skull reflexes and automatic behaviours. Our apparent unreality – our very unreality – witnessed to a self-confessional reality in which we came to the edge of ourselves and looked *through* ourselves. To be true (to know truth) within an age of violence and lies, an age subject to the reflexes of Skull, was to sense a curious irreality in oneself, a curious originality, a curious divergence from the circus of the real (or what passed for the real).

All this made me scan Emma's features closely. She was veiled by dateless day infinity comedy. I saw her innate sorrow. I suddenly saw how worn she was. It was as if a nail had woven its innermost weblike constancy into her flesh, an ecstatic nail, a sorrowing nail. Ecstatic and sorrowing! That was her bizarre truth, her divergence from what passed as the real in the circus of the normal and the real.

'O Emma,' I cried impulsively, 'tell me please. How have you made out all these years? There were debts to pay, the old house was sold. Even Miriam's theatre fell under the hammer though W. H. preserved it for a while.'

'I have paid dearly,' Emma said. 'Survival is dear, it is beyond price, but it is worth it.'

'It must have been a difficult time after Alice's death, Miriam's death, my death.'

'A difficult time indeed,' Emma confessed, 'a difficult adjustment for Peter and me. We once shared everything, remember? We were part of your family, remember? We shared the little theatre in the magic wood, remember? We shared every meal. And then came the earthquake, the crash . . . It was as if we had been orphaned all over again. Flung out of the cradle all over again. But there was no one like Alice to take us in this time. As I lay on the beach I was pierced by the cry of the gulls, the laughing sea gulls. Were they gulls or were they cranes? I could not tell. It was a cry from heaven and yet it was a subtle, piercing, shaking laughter. A shaking note like strings of music in the sea. The motif of an incomparable composition. Music such as we had dreamt to hear in our little theatre.' She stopped as if she remembered something I had forgotten. 'Did you not ask Aunt

Miriam, Robin, what is laughter's mask? Did you not hunt through a trunk of dresses and costumes, etc., in an old cellar?'

'I remember.'

'Aunt Miriam wept when you asked her on the bed of the sea. Well let me tell you, Robin, that the answer lay in a bird's cry, a bird's feather that pierces heaven and strings the music of laughter into the grief of rain. It was a nail, a half-rending sound, that rose from the sea, from *Tiger*'s broken body, from the shattered boat, from the ships of all the navies of all the oceans, from a broken barrel, an invisible barrel on which Alice leaned into the crest of a wave. It was a nail. And it pierced me. I was nailed into the ground.'

'My God, Emma!' I was confused. I recalled the apparition of Ghost, multi-faceted Ghost, innermost Ghost, outermost Ghost, arising from the sea.

'My God, Emma!'

'In such a nail that shatters one's prepossessions I knew the construction of a sound that echoed in the air and in the sea. It was the music of the priest, of the God of nature. One comes,' said Emma, 'to a beloved creation, to the divine, in every moment that one survives in the inimitable textures of nature, truly lives and survives.'

I shook myself hard. I tried to reason with myself. I almost felt that I had taken advantage of her, that I knew her secrets because I had lain with her there on the beach, with my lips within the cover of her hair yet on her breasts. I shook myself. I tried to reason with myself. 'You were desolated, Emma. You had narrowly escaped drowning. One understands.'

'One understands,' said Emma and looked at me as if she were addressing Peter, 'that a priest in a desolate age, in a drowned age, must pay dear for an illumination of ecstasy, Robin. How can one surrender oneself to laughter in the midst of survival that leaves one bereft? How can one sing in the midst of survival that leaves one bereft? How can one play? Yet one does. Peter sings. Peter plays. Calypso sings. Calypso dances. And you and Alice and Miriam paid with your lives for them to be merry in the light of a stranger ecstasy. As for me I became a priest. I dedicated myself to simplicity's tasks, simplicity's meals, and to a butterfly-lantern at the heart of the globe.'

I felt her lips upon mine. The kiss of all loves and all true lovers.

SEVEN

THE SCENE CHANGES. We are now in the elaborate promenade of Prospero Mall. Emma pulls a veil like the sea around her eyes. She slips away but not before depositing a note in the pocket of my coat. I pull it out. The note is faded as if it had been written long, long ago. In an age of childhood when we were encouraged by Miriam and Alice to write letters to one another about fabulous journeys to the ends and the beginnings of time. I smooth the note slowly and read:

Dear Robin,

The next leg of your journey will take you up the Mountain of Folly. And Peter's assistance will prove invaluable. Do not ask me how I know! Let us say we are privy to one another's secrets. We are, if you like, lovers in infinity. When Peter lay beside me on the beach before the ambulance arrived I dreamt it was you! (Aunt Miriam says I am an imaginative letter writer.) What I have to say now will come as a shock. Peter's addicted to three bands in the sacred wood. One is Calypso's and Tiger's band which he joined a year or so after your imaginary (it seems so real now – or is it in the future?) death. The second is called the rocket-crucifixion band. The third is Faust's circus band.

Peter joined the rocket-crucifixion band and Faust's circus band not very long ago and decided not to give his own name this time but to use an alias. Indeed he used your name – Robin Redbreast Glass. A parcel of cheek! Shocking *alter ego* Glass cheek! Faust calls him Robin! So don't be surprised when he addresses *him* by *your* name. Miriam says it's a kind of test between 'remembering' and 'forgetting' when you climb. Peter, of course, chose your name because it was dead simple. He knew everything about you. It was easy to secure your birth certificate and to answer any questions that Faust might ask.

Faust (he calls himself Doctor Faustus in Prospero Mall) has his surgery – as it is called – at the end of the Mall.

Surgery! An odd name, I know, but it relates to Faust's alchemy (Aunt Miriam explained things about alchemy), his phantom nooses, phantom crosses, *and* also (this is important) '*a shift that is occurring in the priorities of Billionaire Death from whom Faust borrows capital to invest in themes of simulated immortality.*' (I have copied this last from a dusty old book that W. H. reads when he assists Aunt Miriam in staging our plays.) The shift – the book goes on to say – in the priorities of Skull extends through all generations. It's a frail shift – the book says – but it may build up suddenly into a creative breakthrough. I like that. Don't you? (W. H. says we are becoming literate imaginations!) The Mountain of Folly, for instance – according to Alice's legend – has been riddled or penetrated by the vision of a hospital of infinity in which refugees of spirit may reside. (I am a bit frightened by all this, aren't you? But excited.)

The book also says that the poor doomed people in our theatre of Skull may no longer be doomed as before, that the hospital of infinity is an unexpected blessing in coming space programmes.

On the other hand I heard Tiger growling, 'it's too damned early to be sure.' Things may slip back again. A lot may depend on you and Peter when you climb the Mountain. It's up to you to save them. And I shall do my best. Remember me.

Emma

PS One thing more. Make your way to Faust's surgery. You will find Peter there and hear news of the rocket band in which (Miriam whispers) Faust has an interest.

I folded the letter with care and replaced it in my pocket. Dateless Day Infinity Road had brought me now to the end of the Mall. I heard Doctor Faustus's voice just above me in the Mountain of Folly.

'Don't fall this time, Robin. Take your time. It's a new invention. It's a new rocket nursery in the stars. A new band blew up above Skull on its way to Mars. Lives were lost. But you can count on me now. So take your time, Robin.'

I was on the point of protesting – 'I am not a member of a rocket band or of Tiger's band for that matter.' And then I recalled Emma's note from long, long ago in Miriam's childhood theatre. How remarkable that a childhood/adolescent love affair should blossom into a female priesthood and nourish the resurrection body. What a shift, a frail shift, yet intimate revolutionary breakthrough into the prospect of a divine Communism in which all generations reflected one another at the heart of anguish yet consummate wisdom.

I recalled Emma's note. Faust was addressing *alter ego* Glass Robin in Peter. And yet was he not also speaking directly to me, my absent body yet dream-presence, dream re-entry into the theatre of life?

'When the rocket blew,' Faust continued, 'it opened like a cross. It tautened into a rope. I saw it through my ancient eyes in the workshop of the gods. My ancient eyes that blaze like a comet at the end of time, the beginning of time. Who can say which end, which beginning? I have forgotten so much, have forfeited so much, to become the comedian of the machine in this end or beginning of time.'

It almost seemed to me as if Faust were pleading with Peter and me. 'It tautened into a marvellous rope, Robin,' he said.

He stared at Peter from his windowsill above the Mall. A wind blew down the Mountain of Folly. The terror of his smile was lost upon Peter but I was aware of it, all the more aware of it after the mystical laughter of which Emma had spoken (our arms around one another by the sea). I saw it lucidly now (as if for a moment I had borrowed Faust's ancient eyes, Faust's remembering/oblique forgetting eyes, Faust's Quetzalcoatl eyes in which were entwined the marriage of heaven and earth). I saw the backward shift, the forward shift, the folly, the creativity, the parallel laughters of the universe, the laughter of grace and mystery for which one pays dear, the laughter of the electric machine, of mechanical stimulation, one buys cheap.

'You know, Robin,' Faust said to Peter, 'I like to think of my surgery as a window upon heaven. Except that heaven's changing. (Indeed the workshop I knew in ancient times has long vanished.) The crucifixion's changing. Technology's changing. And quite frankly I'm not sure what investitures the devil now wears. If there's a shift in the radius of a star, in the radius of the soul, who can say on which side one's bread is buttered?' He pointed to a plate on his windowsill and I read: *Doctor Faustus, fallen angel from the workshop of the gods, ambivalent sceptic of the purposes of evil, reluctant doctor of the soul.* He was smiling with the blandness of his forgetting/remembering eyes and I felt a chill. 'I am on Emma's side, Robin,' he said.

He saw my disbelief and continued to press his argument. *My* disbelief? No, Peter's. 'For the fact is, Robin, if I'm not careful I shall have nothing to work with – the materials I employ will become sterile – I shall lose everyone and everything. And live in an empty shell from which labour has vanished, machines doing everything, thinking machines, acting machines, killing machines. And so let's seek a lull in our space wars on earth and in heaven. A respite from computer voices and computer generals and computer admirals in the twenty-first century. Let's give ourselves a chance to define our terms anew, rehearse the technologies of the crucifixion. Turn them round and round, upside down, downside up, make a rope, a rope and a rocket cross into heaven.'

I saw he was playing with Peter, playing with some ancient design of hope he may have abandoned. He was wooing him with the irreverence, the self-mocking humour, for which the comedian of the machine was universally famous. He knew he was taking a risk, that there might be something in what he was saying that Peter might remember and take to heart but this was a chance he had to accept on behalf of the new spatial cross of humanity. 'Come, come, Robin,' he said to Peter, 'I'm on your side, believe me. We're making the world safe for mankind. I'm up here to receive you. You've hesitated long enough. Seize the glory rope and climb into heaven. I promise you no one will burn this time.'

I kept still and virtually invisible beside Peter like a child playing hide-and-seek in a resurrection cupboard. I saw what Emma had meant. I saw the curious pitch, the curious darkness of a spiritual irony within a destitute world enriched by the oddest parallels, sophisticated technologies running side by side with rickety cupboards, barrels, worn blankets, sheets, chalk to make a seam or line on diagrams of the sky and the sea depicting the intimate recesses of 'remembering' and 'forgetting' – all substance of the shoestring budget of childhood theatre.

Priorities were changing but so peculiarly, so involuntarily it seemed, that the resurrection body could easily be lured from its true seam or true line in the heart of creation with promises that only It (masked Peter and masked me and others of linked generations) could make valid in the light of the rehearsed values within the deaths of Alice and Miriam and grandfather and others lying in the refugee sea or in the refugee forest or up in the refugee stars (their untenanted graves memorialized in a pork-knocker barrel on earth).

For we had been empowered in our nursery rhymes to weigh the doors and windows of heaven, to knock on them and seek assurances of the nature and the meaning of value.

What was the true seam or the true line that Peter and I needed to understand in our ascent and our overcoming of the Mountain of Folly?

I gave Peter a slight nudge and at last he gripped the rope and began to ascend to Doctor Faustus's surgery. He drew close to the windowsill. Faust leaned out to seize him. I shouted.

'Peter,' I cried (and forgot to call him Robin), 'swing away from the rope or the cross to the true seam in the wave of rock.'

My forgetfulness in this instance may have saved Peter's life. Faust hesitated for a fraction of an instant. He had heard my voice as if it came from nowhere yet from another source, another line, another thread in space. He was taken aback by all this (by the repudiation of his deadly rope) and by the name 'Peter' of which he was unaware. He knew only of 'Robin'. Who was Peter? Nobody (or absent body) was Peter. Impossible parallels! And in that flash of lightning bemusement that fell over the Mountain of Folly Peter slipped from Faust's grasp as if he were made of Glass: made of *alter ego* Robin Glass, *alter ego* kingdoms of space.

As he gained the seam or divide in the wave of rock I remembered my earliest temptations threaded into the first time I dreamt I heard voices and sounds. I remembered how I had succumbed to the temptation to seize the kingdoms of space. Had I then – without knowing it – stored up a shift in the priorities of life and death? Had I anticipated Faust in miniaturizing the creation in myself? Had I been in league with my grandfather's revisionary book as I now stood in league with Emma's Peter? I had stored, I felt now, in frail treaty with the past and the future, a lightning caution by which or through which to outwit the comedian of the machine when he sought to pull all generations into a window of heaven that was ambiguous if not false, an enchainment of the mind if not an extinction of the soul.

A political parable of mind and soul born of childhood

remembered visions in an age of dangerous superpowers professing the good intention out of cunning self-interest, the good life out of expedient design.

Peter and I pursued the seam in the wave of rock until a glimmering window in the Mountain of Folly, like a flag one sticks on the moon beneath a black sky, and a white imaginary sea spelt our approach to a ward in space from which Billionaire Death inspected the cosmos. His imaginary eyes met mine. They were shockingly large and black and deep as if I mistook a West Indian black-coated vista of Mars for Columbus's Venusian India. I tried to adjust my world-weary resurrected gaze within those imaginary eyes. I dreamt I saw them change and turn subtly green, subtly marvellous within love's murmuring death wish on earth ascending to the hospital of space. I thought of sunset as if it had been painted on a child's ball in the depths of space at the heart of a long summer vanished day when imaginary veil upon veil of light *speaks* of the birth of unremembered glory. I thought of the imagination of twilight at the heart of equatorial sunset and the cry of a vanished bird when the rustle of wings ties one's breath into a feather that floats unconsumed into the darkness.

I thought of the sensation of pain and of benevolent oblivion. I was confused, bewildered, by a sensation of music, a sensation of beauty (as if an unwritten symphony shrouded my eyes, unwitting revolutionary creativity entertained by Billionaire Death). And I recalled Emma's perception of laughter's mask as she lay in my arms by the sea. Her perception, I knew, was also saturated by the imaginary cry of an incredible bird born in the workshop of heaven at its margins with the waste land. And I was struck now in Billionaire Death's presence by what seemed an intermediate vibration between parallel musics of which I already knew: Emma's dear music of mystery and grace and the cheap music of the electric machine in the circus of hell. *Now* – between these parallels that were so unlike one another – lay the imaginary chord I had glimpsed in Billionaire Death's eyes. *Love's death wish.* It was as if in seeing this, hearing this, I glimpsed again a reluctant shift in the priorities of life and death.

'Life is blind spirit, death is love,' Billionaire Death said in the voice of a strange organ. I knew I must shake off the dreadful fascination and responded almost without thinking: 'One needs to convert love's death wish into generations that are capable of such intimate rapport with one another's frailties that love leads them *through* death not *into* oblivion's space adventure. Life leads them into spirit as if the passage through spirit is the infinity of invisible spirit itself.'

Billionaire Death turned from me to Peter. He knew my voice. He remembered the voice that had addressed Peter and outwitted Doctor Faustus. He felt the time had come to make me aware of his wealth and his power.

'I have received billions and trillions to gain the eyes I possess.'

'You mean you are rich enough to have *paid* or spent billions . . .'

'Not so. *Received*. Death never pays. Death receives. My eyes reflect the accumulated receipt of love's death wish. My eyes are the substance of all atmospheres that pour into me. I do not spend, Robin. I receive. The cheaper life is, the greater the undervaluation of the mystery of life – the more it sings to me in all sorts of fashions and follies, the more it grieves for me – the less it resists theatres of extinction and the destruction of species and populations.

'Who really cares, Robin, how vast are the sums civilization devotes to weapons of destruction? Life is cheap, so spend, spend, spend on fashions of death becomes the refrain that falls into me and fills my treasury.'

He paused and placed upon me the imaginary and brooding vistas of his unwritten music in which I saw through his eyes the terrible opera of an age. 'From the last two World Wars alone I pocketed billions of royalty. Calculate the astronomical sums spent on the war poems written in the trenches! How much did it cost civilization to bring a handful of poets there and throw a sunset/sunrise blanket over their eyes? I plucked those eyes out of their heads and planted them in mine.

'Imagine what it costs Redbreast Robin to maim a child or a man or a woman in a bombed city. I have reaped imaginary harvests and Ghost knows what in Vietnam and the Lebanon.' He turned and pointed to an imaginary bed on which I dreamt I saw three children dressed in Alice's masks – the mask of Beirut, the mask of Belfast, the mask of Jamaica. They oscillated or stirred in the hospital of infinity.

He saw me staring at the Jamaican mask. 'Oh that! Just a

pittance. People were stoning one another and the little female mask ran on the battleground and was killed. How much did it bring? Let's see.' He plucked a blur of stones from his brow and chest. Blurred stones in the photography of pupil and orb in Death's majestic eyes. Jagged. Sharp. They had cut to the brain. I looked at the child again and wondered whether she had seized love's death wish with her last breath.

'You said a pittance,' I spoke helplessly. 'Just a pittance.'

'Oh yes, a pittance,' Billionaire Death repeated. 'Let's see.' He adjusted his imaginary eyes and I saw angry bodies breaking a surf of cane and vegetables upon a glowing hillside. Their arms were slashed but it did not matter. I saw hands coated with dust digging the sun from the hillside. The broken stones from the hillside lost their glow as they were lifted and flung.

'Say five hundred dollars for loss of crops,' said Billionaire Death, 'their loss, my gain. Twenty dollars for each hillside stone. A stone has fossil value in geologic space. A score of stones. Twenty by twenty. Four hundred dollars. Five plus four. Nine hundred dollars. Make it a round sum for a child's life – a thousand dollars. *Death's a banker, life's a . . . life's a . . . life's a . . . life's a bloody pauper.*' His voice, I suddenly realized, seemed to have stuck in his throat. A hiccup of a song in a child's breaking breast.

Yo-ho-ho and a bottle of rum.

EIGHT

Death pulled the window down upon the frightful scene and brawl I had witnessed through his eyes. But not before leaving on the windowsill a pair of glittering scales and the stone from the hillside that had killed a child. Peter and I placed Alice's ring on one scale and the stone on the other. They drew level in perfect equilibrium, perfect equality in the heart of light.

'I wonder,' I said to Peter, 'what Death received on behalf of Alice and Miriam the afternoon they drowned? (And I with them?) It couldn't have been much. Alice had spent virtually every penny. And there were debts as you know. Miriam's little theatre would have fetched but a pittance. Yes . . .' I found myself brooding on the word *pittance*, 'just a pittance.'

I stopped. Peter was silent.

'Do you know,' I said, 'when we drew level with Billionaire Death's hospital and treasury I remembered my pork-knocker library, every morsel and text into which I dug. I used to play, remember, I was a grave-digger in the magic wood. What are those books worth now? Another pittance.'

'Enough,' said Peter, 'to bring me a bed in space. And the flavour of being cared for and caring for others. Books of a certain kind – written and revised (as you would say) by the hand of the magical dead – have anti-gravity substance. Death may laugh at them but they have a place, an original place, on his scales.'

I scarcely heard what he was saying except that my books had secured him a bed in space. 'You?' I demanded. 'Bought you a bed?'

'Why yes me and *alter ego* you in a manner of speaking, Robin,' said Peter mildly. 'How could I be here ascending the Mountain of Folly, how endure its riddles in the heart of a dying age, except I had died to the machinations of Skull? A creative dying! A shared mask with the dying living in every theatre of conscience. *Emma's alive*. She wears the mask of an archbishop in AD 2025. Her coronation's today. Eighty years old. She like ourselves was born in 1945 when the Bomb fell.'

'But when I dreamt I saw you and her in the tunnel . . . She dropped an ancient letter in my pocket and you were a book in her hand whose pages she turned . . .'

'You were digging in your library and theatre of Sleep, Robin. You saw her through Death's quantum eyes. And the quantum imagination risks everything to know the truth. Death becomes something of a classic when we fictionalize it, the classic penetration of all our ills and a revolutionary moment in our submission to the resurrection.'

'You have not understood, Peter!' I cried. 'I am saying that when I saw her I sensed something, I sensed a struggle with ancient plays and texts and letters – I knew she was worn – she confessed her difficulties of an intimate nature – but she seemed so incredibly close to my immortal youth, immortal drowned Glass youth and mirror of space through which all things flit in the alchemy of the imagination.'

'I know, I know, immortal Robin. The machinations of Faust. Beware of the Glass that may mesmerize you. And yet in another light immortality is the comedy of a changeless romance between true, inner flesh and true, outer spirit. Immortality is a feather in the Nightfall of the sea and the land. A feather by which we know that a stone and a ring and other relics that seem unequal may float and link themselves into a chain. Infinity's chain. That that chain remains unbroken despite everything is our slender passion and hope of the transformation of injustice that we inflict on ourselves and upon others. Should it sever then we are lost. Then we fall into the abyss. But it will not, it cannot.'

His words were the cue for us to move up to another room in space. Ghost had given this ward or room to his chauffeur of infinity who was tinkering at this moment with the rocket of which Doctor Faustus had spoken, the rocket band that had fallen from the sky.

'It's a fast car,' I said to Peter. 'It's a still drum or band or something yet it's moving at a fantastic speed. How can anyone hold on and work! Gravity's – anti-gravity's – miracle. I see it as if my eyes are glued into a camera yet flying in a moving fast photographic lens and object in a dark night beyond Mars and Venus.'

'Planets are ailing fast cars in the hospital of infinity. They've been struck by giant meteors. A meteor's a BOOM, BOOM,

DOOM, DOOM band. This rocket fell at the foot of the Mountain of Folly. Then it was transported here. And it's flying still on a film. Such is the genius of Faust.' Peter was joking with his usual solemn, long face that I knew from long, long ago when we drew planets with chalk on blackboard in Miriam's childhood theatre.

'Each planet is the car of an imaginary greatness. Greatness rides again in the West! If you and I sit still, Robin, and wait long enough we may enter into orbit with Alexander and Napoleon and Captain Cat from *Under Milk Wood*.'

'Captain Cat is crying,' I said. 'Do you remember that line? Captain Cat is dancing to the music of a sad Rosy guitar.'

'Napoleon's too fat to dance. The car or the ship or the chariot or the planet on which he lies is a dusty or a waterlogged campaign. It needs to be refurbished with glory. And as a consequence Ghost is driven to employ an army of doctors, chauffeurs of infinity, engineers, programmers, etc., etc., to build new beds, new experimental bunks in tanks, in submarines, in aeroplanes. New cannon poking out of featherbed pillows.'

'Employment,' I cried, 'it's employment for millions.' But then I was stricken by the unemployment of the soul. 'What is greatness,' I asked Peter, 'if the soul itself falls into disuse?'

'And another thing,' I said, 'where lies the unbroken chain, the slender hope of which you spoke, in the débâcle of greatness that threatens to break the back of the earth?'

'It lies in this seam we are pursuing *through* the Mountain of Folly,' said Peter. 'Look! Captain Cat is dancing. Old as a crafty waste land seer but not fat.' And as he spoke I remembered the lament of Tiger and Calypso in the magic wood. I also remembered *Tiger*, Alice's boat, that had toppled into the breaking sea. I remembered Tiresias, the seer, whose spectacles I now placed on my eyes like a tourist under a black sky. I saw the negative film of Thebes, I saw the negative film of ancient walls under the sea through which *Tiger* fell. I saw Napoleon's negative crown and Alexander's sceptre and Captain Cat's tombstone floating with Alice's ring and with the stone from a Jamaican hillside. Except that they lay now far below the wave on the glittering scales that the fictionalization of Death had brought to me.

It was an uncanny vortex. The flotsam and jetsam of empires! Everything moving fast yet still. Everything balanced yet toppling.

'All I can say,' I began but stopped and appealed to Ghost. He saw my plight and put words on the page of my lips.

'All I can say is that the scales are set to weigh an imaginary substance, the imaginary substance of greatness that lies in a fabric we can never wholly grasp.

'When I saw the ring and the stone in equilibrium at Death's window I was involved in a religious equation between violence (the slain child) and sacrament (the ring). It was as if the speeding universe slowed for a moment into marvellous poise and equilibrium of spirit within relics of memory. But higher up now – with Ghost's chauffeur – I cannot dodge or escape the fact of chaos (and so must relate to it as a factor in the marvellous equation of spirit): must relate to it through history that expands into the vision of the seer, visionary motion in motionlessness, the ironies of full employment yet the unemployment of the soul; and this involves me as much in the day I was drowned – when the boat *Tiger* sank – as in the day ancient Rome fell or Byzantium became a mirage and Greece vanished.

'Imagine the refugees of spirit across the centuries. Imagine the marriage of turbulence and stillness in every dying mask, imagine vast waves and still bodies, moving hordes and etched caravans against a sky that topples into space. Imagine the literacy of the seer at the heart of chaos, a literacy that reads the beauty of God in every delicate web within the seamless robe of eternity.'

Seam and seamlessness! Peter and I had pursued the seam or the delicate web between remembering and forgetting faculties in our ascent *through* and *above* the Mountain of Folly. *Through* and *above*! *Within* and *without*! Here lay the paradox of the seamless garment upon Emma's shoulders. Peter vanished. I thought I saw him ascending the wave of the rock and then it was as if his shadow melted into the air.

'I shall take you through the city,' Tiresias said, 'to Emma's coronation. It's quite an event. Sculpture, song, dance. Millions all over the world, in villages, on mountaintops, in valleys, in bars, in hotel rooms, may be able to view it. I shall take you in a little while. I am not sure her brother Peter fully approves. After all he is her twin. He played in Tiger's band. He became the pope of the calypso. An odd title I know. But it's common knowledge that the calypsonian bands adorn themselves with curious titles. The name I bear (Tiresias) figures as you know and once or twice I have danced with them, danced the dance of the twining snakes, half-man, half-woman. The seer needs to know, to see everything from within the heart of chaos – if that is at all possible.'

'You were speaking,' I said, 'of the bands.'

'Ah yes, the bands! There's the black Napoleon band. There's the Persian Ayatollah Alexander band. There's Peter's band. Indeed, as I said before, he was the pope of the bands in Skull until his death the afternoon that you met him in the tunnel. Emma would tell you he had been ailing for some time. Ailing science, ailing religion. No wonder Doctor Faustus warned him of a meteor rocket, a meteor drum, falling from heaven. Part of his trouble was that he was a bit of a woman-hater. A long-standing taint in the body of our civilization. It fouls the nest of religion. And of economics though you wouldn't think it at first. But what is the soul of the unemployed but an implicit extension of the whoredom of money we cultivate subconsciously? I tried, therefore, to mediate between him and the whoredom of money long, long ago – when Greece and Rome were doomed – by egging on Frog to play an inferior modern Ulysses and magistrate and pygmy shadow of the giant of the heartland.

'In that way I involved *you*, Robin Redbreast Glass, as the son and the heir of a divided tradition. It was the best I could do in the licentious theatre of Skull. Thus it was that I edged myself into half-man, half-woman masks (even Ghost is not immune to such masquerades) in my mimicry, in my rehearsals, of divine equilibrium that is beyond our grasp. All this, by the way, is implicit in Emma's book which she attempted to read to you in staggered passages when you met in Dateless Infinity Day in your dream. Emma's theology vindicated my and Ghost's disguises. It is rooted in the necessity to bring a sacramental urgency to the ancient and perennially fertile body of sex. Not promiscuity, not cheap stimulation. But something we scarcely understand. The miracle of the senses, touch, taste, echoing waves and particles and penetration.

'Her task, from this day forward, is *to make the body of the resurrection beautiful to the woman in the man, the man in the woman.* It's a formidable vocation. *You* should know that, Robin. You lay with your head on her breasts by the sea.'

'Was it not Peter who lay with her? I was drowned, Peter had been saved.' *And yet, even as I spoke, I did seem to remember . . .*

'Peter, yes, but your shadow slowly took shape out of every refugee of spirit. Took infinite and rehearsible form. It drew Peter into imitating you. He took your name, remember? Alias Robin Redbreast Glass. He was universally popular in Skull in love's death-wish bands. All fanaticism is rooted subconsciously in love's terrible death wish! But by degrees you triumphed. Your original sensuousness, your true passion, triumphed. And by the time Emma came to write her intimate book of you and Peter after your death it was *you* she drew into her arms. Your true passion in nature. And then by degrees in your ascent of the Mountain Peter himself – despite his discomfiture, his reservations – was imbued by the miracle of equilibrium between all genders, all opposites.

'I put it crudely of course. But you know the subtleties of chaos and history that you have drawn into yourself Robin Redbreast Glass. Peter too was converted but he's her brother. He's fixated in a kind of incest. When brothers and sisters marry – whatever the traditional or dogmatic excuse – it's incest. Or if not incest it's purity masturbating. And there's been enough of that I say from my standpoint in the underworld. And that's where I come in as your guide, Robin, on this day. You need to descend from the Mountain and to start from below in your voyage into a new unity.'

I looked up the Mountain. I missed Peter. I missed the pope of love's death wish. I had never, I confessed to myself, seen him in that light in the magic wood or in the theatre of an infinite rehearsal of values but I was now prepared to accept the guidance of the stranger seer who stood between the deformities of the popular religion of the bands and the sacrament of sensuous marriage between heaven and earth for which I had suffered in the sea and on the land.

Tiresias led me down the Mountain along the other side of the seam and within the hospital of infinity. I caught a glimpse of ailing stars, of meteors gouging holes in planets, of ailing moons and constellations, of ailing civilizations far out in space whose residual and imaginary glow had been simulated by Doctor Faustus, the reluctant doctor of the soul.

We came down to Skull with a bump. Not with a bang but with a bump like a boat that oscillates in a wave. The streets were swarming with refugees of soul and spirit, refugees of heart and mind. And my first vision was of the Beast with the map of heaven in its claws or its hands. No, *his* claws, *his* hands.

I had seen the Beast before when I hid Ghost in my shadow and outwitted Frog. But in this instance or imminent rehearsal of values he seemed quite different. I dreamt he turned his gaze upon me as if he remembered me from the day I was born. And I drifted into his psychical glass eyes and perceived the vortex of the Tiresian dance. It was the dance of bone and flesh within and without the Beast in the mystery of the resurrection body. I was aware of the wreck of *Tiger* in the mirror of the sea beside the magic wood. The vortex grew steady as a rock. The vortex was a sleeping, spinning, steady top in my dream.

The crew upon *Tiger* were masked in bone as they danced.

'You have seen them before, these dancers,' said Tiresias, 'in your grandfather's pork-knocker theatre of great navigators and conquistadores. Becalmed above an impossible garden.'

'But this is *Tiger*,' I said, 'the wreck of *Tiger* beside the magic wood and under the sea. This is – or was – my grave.'

'All graves are becalmed vessels above an impossible garden. Until I mediate in the underworld and sprinkle the lips of bone with Beast-food. So I repeat, Robin Glass, you have seen them before. You saw them the moment you died. I moistened your eyes then with an appetite for visions. And the grain of all foundered ships came alive. You have seen them before I say – the crew of bone that fish for a morsel, a Beast-morsel, Beast-fish, Beast-grain, Beast-shrimp.'

I dreamt I now saw Alice and Miriam on the deck of the Beast-ship of life under the sea. They were masked in flesh. Not bone. But as I scanned their curious bodies in 'sleeping top' dance of *stillness* and flesh with sailors of bone I saw the stillness for what it was. *Stillness* was a 'hole' in each body through which I looked beyond the dance into vistas of oceanic spirit. There was a shout like a hoarse drum and one of the bone sailors heaved upon his fishing rod and drew in his line. Beast-fish at last! They cooked and ate. As the fire subsided in the orchestra of the sea, and the spray darkened into musical coal, I was startled profoundly by another 'hole' in Miriam's body. The bone-sailors in their dance, in eating the fish, had subtly cannibalized the spectre of death and eaten into the gravity – or the anti-gravity – of Miriam's flesh, animal flesh, female flesh. Eaten into the dance and into themselves as well, into their male bone and acquired in consequence a crack or tooth-mark, a sparkling intensity or flute of soul.

And I recalled the tooth of creation that I had brought with me from a sparkling wave when I arose from the sea. I had not understood its innermost music of appetite for vision until now as I moved in the Glass and the mirror of the Beast with the map of heaven in its hands.

'The resurrected body consumes a vision in every morsel of meat or fish it reflects or cooks,' said Tiresias. 'For every disciple of vision dies and dies again and again with an ailing creation. One dies because one lives a visionary life beyond the cannibal consumption of dancing grain, dancing fruit, dancing flesh. The gardens of the Beast are signposted with visionary signals of death and resurrection in the agriculture of the soul, the hunting grounds of the soul that loom in the stylized drink and the stylized meat of the soul.'

As he spoke I remembered the unemployed soul of humanity in the stylized munition factories of Skull. What stylized teeth and jaws did such an unemployed soul wear? Were they stylized iron teeth, stylized iron jaws, with little or no apprehension of the dead shrimp in a mouth chewing aimlessly, violently? I saw the stylized body of the unemployed soul of humanity turning within a deeper and deeper chaos of insensible vision, a deeper and deeper blindness, a deeper and deeper grave.

'Visionary employment beyond the grave,' said Tiresias (and I wondered in what degree he was mocking all civilizations), 'is an alteration in the biases of the soul, it is a threshold into the resurrection of the body.'

Were not mockery and self-mockery a measure in themselves of the changing shroud, the changing investitures, of bias? I saw all at once – in the psychical Glass eyes in which I stood within the giant grave of the underworld – that the Beast was involved in weaving a portion of Emma's seamless garment and that such a weave was a pointer into the tasks of the employed soul.

I followed the light, almost invisible, thread along *Tiger*'s deck and into every minuscule eye of bone, every faint crack, every 'hole' in the flesh of the vortex, the spinning top of sleep in the garden of the remembered sea, every fissure, every sailor, until I was aware of its still match within the flame and the bite of the water, within the flame and the bitten water, as if the light thread turned on itself into an intricate reversal of expectations.

When *Tiger* sailed Alice and Miriam and I and the others who were drowned that day had invested in a safe return to harbour. When Navies sail the crew invest in a safe return to harbour. When civilizations harness the swamp or the earthquake-hillside or the volcanic plateau, humanity invests in safe walls and cities. How safe? How doomed? That the Beast had spun its portion of Emma's seamless robe in such a context was a pointer into the choices one makes (or which one should perceive one is involved in making), the price one pays at every level of existence (or may find one is called upon to pay when one lives by choice apparently on the edge of the abyss).

'The Beast-thread in the vortex and the stillness is the life of the *dear* seed one should visualize as a warning of the spirit against monstrous excess, the life of *dear* energy one should visualize as an illumination of true body and mind (a grain of light in a dark world is sustenance indeed), the life of the *dear* corn, the *dear* flower, the *dear* fruit, one should read with the eyes of the heart and the mind as frail extensions of the body of the earth, the convulsive power of the body of the earth that writes of itself with ecstatic petal or cloth of beauty by which it heals its ceaseless ailments and sustains its paradoxical fertility.

'The life of the dear seed in a blind world intent on excess, addicted to excess, addicted to poverty as much as to glamour, sharpens, I fear,' said the seer of the underworld, 'the edge of overturned expectations, the edge of terror in cities, the edge of terrifying pathos in cultures doomed by nature itself, if nature is to survive as a phenomenon of value and therapy of the blind soul.

'True survival costs dear, Robin Redbreast Glass, true survival should measure its technologies, its investments, against the light of an overturning of expectations and within a capacity to look and move beyond immediate place, immediate time. True survival should be aware of the temptations of prosperity in fabulous ghettos, fabulous concentration camps. True survival should measure the price we have begun to pay to the Beast in the garden of life as we gambol with it, dance with it, and exploit it to our apparent heart's content.'

NINE

The dance of the vortex staged by the Tiresias Tiger band was now over and I found myself once again in the throngs of Skull. I was aware of the divisions in the population. There were the doomsters and the boomsters. Skull was doomed (that was the logic of the doomsters). Skull was invincible concentration camp (that was the message of the boomsters). They sang together DOOM, DOOM, BOOM, BOOM. I stood amongst them with the unfinished thread Beast had woven reflected in my Glass. Unfinished climax with Being. Unfinished thread that ran through the recesses of merriment to illumine all the more vividly the divisions of which I was aware in every city, every village, that floated before me in the panorama of Tiresias.

'And both,' said the seer of the underworld, 'both groups, doomsters and boomsters, must suffer the reversal of expectation. You will not see Emma today, Robin Redbreast Glass. The climax between yourself and the new priest, the new archbishop, remains in suspension. Until humanity can gauge its defeats and the reversed sail by which it moves, one hopes, towards a philosophy of true survival.' There was a clamour in the air, horns and trumpets and drums that issued from the recesses of existence.

'What is true survival?' I said in dismay as if even I (the resurrected body) had forgotten everything the dark seer had said. I looked for Emma but she was not to be seen.

'You must sail towards her,' said Tiresias. 'Have I not already implied what true survival is?'

He paused for a fraction and considered. 'Let me rehearse again before I vanish some of the implications of true survival. To sail in the nuclear rigging of Skull – in anticipation of the raising of *Tiger* and its reversed sail – is to sight all the more vividly the earthquake regions or the volcanic regions or the flood regions or the famine/drought regions of the earth.

'Not that I, Tiresias, need any reminder. Over the centuries it has been my lot to patrol wrecked villages and cities and pastures where dead sheep nibble the lava from the sun in a mountain top.

'It has been my lot to mediate between all expectations. And in the teeth of flame I have learnt that someone always survives, some group always survives. The survivors may come (it is ironical) from those who lived in the expectation of doom. Equally many who vanish may have been possessed by a conviction of infallible ground. I – as their mediator – had no alternative but to encompass all groups in the underworld and stress a reversed sail, and a spiritual necessity to look into the heart of true survival, into a shadow linking those who were apparently saved and those who were apparently not.

'I attempt, shall I say, to sow a seed in the survivor that runs through his reversed expectation of doom into the shadow of the non-survivor. It is as if they embrace like man and woman and the shadow comes into the light. It is indeed a seed or frail bond between light and shadow, a frail window of strangest flesh-and-blood between the visible and the invisible. That seed is the primitive impulse of the resurrection of the body. For how can there be a true resurrection without a true balance between opposites by which we measure the human in the divine, the divine in the human? To measure or weigh ourselves against the light-in-the-shadow, the shadow-in-the-light of others is to deepen a reality that breaches the ailing premises of time.'

Tiresias stopped.

'This is as far as I – the mediator in every crisis of expectation – may go with you, Robin Redbreast Glass. I illumine the seed of fire to enhance the regeneration of wheat. I illumine the shifting plates within the globe to engage civilizations in movements and migrations of threatened peoples and species upon an earth that is still the nursery of hope. In the fire of spirit let us wrest a therapy of the heart and the mind. Let us steep every inch of the resurrection in a capacity to weigh a reversed sail that arises and moves above the seas of chaos.'

It was his last word. He vanished, it seemed, upon the blowing of a horn or the roll of a drum.

I stood still amongst the moving pageants and throngs. I held the unfinished thread in the Glass of spirit. I remembered Canterbury in the magic wood of childhood, the play of Canterbury that Miriam and Alice had written and which Peter and I and other children had performed when we crowned Emma in our little theatre. The little theatre of remembered/forgotten history one encompasses in a lifetime but must pursue into the future with reversed sail.

I turned another page in my fictional autobiography. A blank page upon which I had not yet written. Whose hand would seek mine, whose mask become my age in the future? I saw a shadow upon the page, I saw an extension from Ghost. Spirit is one's ageless author, ageless character, in the ceaseless rehearsal, ceaseless performance, of the play of truth. The fictionalization of the self in age and in youth is a multi-faceted caution of the universal imagination against the tyranny of hard, partial fact.

A wave arose that bore me up. Bore the drowned boat up from the sea-bed. I was launched upon my voyage towards Emma.

POSTSCRIPT
BY
GHOST

AD 2025 REMEMBER ME

When Robin set sail I returned to the sea from whence I had come. I am the ghostly voyager in time, in space, in memory, but always I return to the vast ocean, the rolling seas and the great deeps.

I converse now with the mind and the hand of the new mid-twenty-first-century drowned voyager who is to be reflected in Redbreast Glass. Young in mind he shall be as Alice's son was. And his hand? It shall swim both wet and dry as it turns W. H.'s drifting narrative to the stars, drifting between worlds. It shall weigh the obvious with care. For the obvious is sometimes an elusive reality.

'Is there anybody there?' said the drowned voyager,
  Knocking on the moonlit ship . . .
'I am here, I am Ghost, as Robin sails. Listen!'

He listened with a strange ear, a seeing ear, a listening eye, as we tossed on a wave. I gathered together the fragments of a history . . .

W. H. sold Miriam's theatre in the nineteen-sixties (close on three-quarters of a century ago). He sold when others were shouting 'independence and prosperity'. Alice's and Miriam's untimely deaths had left a mortgage on house and theatre. Had they lived that mortgage could have been concealed for a decade or two. In that sense W. H. was ahead of his time. Fate drove him to discharge a debt of tradition while others were basking still in a dubious El Dorado.

What he could not foresee was the moment when Billionaire Death would be driven to loosen his purse strings and multiply the proceeds from the sale of the magic theatre a thousandfold and more to finance the salvage of the wreck of the boat *Tiger*.

This compulsion upon Billionaire Death was astonishing. It sprang from the nerve-end of the resurrection body – the thread of divinity's nerve through all the cavities and the chasms of nature – a nerve-end (or nerve-beginning) that spelt a complex revival of buried resources arching through many cultures and civilizations towards a true voice, a true ear, a true dialogue that the resurrection body nourishes as its ultimate originality. Here at last W. H. felt he could face the world with a dialectic of psyche and imagination. Here at last he saw how Alice's and Miriam's debts drew him to look with uncanny laughter and sorrow into the meaning of the economy he served. To see the mortgage as a debt to sorrow and ecstasy – a debt to (or of) tradition – was to sight and to weave a thread that ran back into the past as it moved into the cross-cultural humanities of the future.

'IT IS A NERVE OR A THREAD IN THE FABRIC OF A SEAMLESS ROBE FAR OUT UPON THE WATERS OF SPIRIT TO WHICH ONE MOVES (I MOVE IN YOU, YOU IN ME) BY INFINITE DEGREES.' Thus I impelled him to dream as I lay within his shadow. Thus I impel *you* to dream as I converse with the future . . .

May I pause and reflect again upon the obvious. I am Ghost. I have never before written a line. But I did utter certain cautionary fragments of text to Robin in the magic wood some time after he hid me in his shadow from the immigration officer Ulysses Frog. If I do write now I do not claim to be original but to tap the innermost resources of eclipsed traditions in the refugee voices that W. H. heard in the sea. I counsel you likewise – with whom I specifically converse – to remember the scripts of foaming water (foaming with constellations) within the traceries of the skeleton marches of the sea. And through these, and this fictional autobiography, I write to you of a seamless robe but find it necessary to stress that such seamlessness is not to be equated with the bounty of conquest. Rather its fabric lies in the spinning vortex of the sea, the still vortex of the sea; as if the still vortex of air, earth and sky – the spinning vortex of dream – secretes a corridor or passageway through every wave and overturning of rigid expectation.

I write in a wave that capsizes into a deformity of vision possessing such ascendancy it tends to conceal its hollowness. Think of that hollow wave as a debt to space! As the fee many a poor soul paid for a ticket to paradise. In the reversal of that hollow wave, space becomes an asset in breaking moulds of prepossession.

It is as if the bill of sale of the magical theatre of childhood that W. H. enacted becomes the currency of spirit. Money is the hurricane that may subside nevertheless into a gentle spray in a realm of ancestral yet new-born space or it is nothing. It may drive a hard bargain between the dead sailor and the living pilot, or a compassionate bargain between the born and the unborn navigator, but its true myth and value lie on the scales of the sea it may never dispense with within a revivification of the spaces of meaning that tie one voyaging generation to another.

How can one sell or put a price on the map of heaven, the map of earth, without incurring an irony that multiplies the purse strings of Billionaire Death? Think of this – you with whom I converse – as you look back from your ship of life and death to the dunning world you have left behind, the landlord or landlady, the butcher, the baker, the candlestick-maker, etc., etc.

As the hollow wave breaks, the chorus of the world becomes all at once a sacramental self-confession.

Robin Redbreast Glass began his voyage towards Archbishop Emma in the year of grace AD 2025 in which I am now writing to you. He carried with him a portion of the seamless robe she is to wear. I plucked it from Beast and gave it to him.

Beast's thread is the seamless garment one carries in ailing nature yet seeks from another source (a healing or healed source) upon the waters of spirit. Carries through arts of sorrow towards the consummation of bliss.

How to find a true balance between such carrying in vessels of nature and such seeking from vessels of spirit!

A wave arises. Look! Here are the scales that Billionaire Death offered Robin and Peter: scales upon which to weigh Alice's ring against the killing stone from a hillside. Look! Do they not compose a perfect match? The stone is purged of terror in the ring of a sacrament upon the scales on the waters of healing spirit.

But alas the stone begins to drift away from the ring into the Night of civilization. As they drift, the thread one carries towards the thread one seeks, appears to be broken or lost.

And yet it remains, it exists. But I, Ghost, know now – I cannot deceive you – that the price to be paid to gain and re-gain such a perception of a balance between 'terror' and 'sacrament' is greater than one imagines. It is a price that may redeem the sale of the earth and the sky in our nuclear age, our nuclear pawnshop, by drawing us – you and me – to the nerve-end fabric in the resurrection body where it touches the sliced purse strings of Billionaire Death.

Weigh that slice against the apparent severance of reality in the thread one carries towards the thread one seeks.

And perhaps one may see again in another light the infinite rehearsal in the economy of the resurrected body, an economy that may still, despite everything, salvage a civilization . . .

On one scale lies the terror of the broken thread or the drifting stone, the explosive rocket, in the seamless garment of God. On the other the sliced purse strings of Billionaire Death.

It is an extreme balance, an extreme purgation of terror in sacramentalized money, in an extreme age. Another wave arises as I address you. Remember me, remember Ghost.